A date with disaster . . .

"Carrie!" her mom called from the front door. "Come on, honey. The guests are already here."

"You want me to leap for joy?" Carrie muttered under her breath.

"Carrie, I told you not to wear black today," Mrs. Mersel hissed in a low whisper. "Melissa is dressed so nicely—"

"Good for her, Mom," Carrie said, stepping into the hallway. She mustered up the biggest smile she could, then turned to face the two people sitting on the lone peach-colored couch in the living room. "Hi—"

She froze, and her jaw dropped.

No, she thought, utterly horrified. *Not her . . .*

Well, well, well.

One thing was for sure. Carrie would not become lifelong friends with this girl.

She could rule out something else, too: All of The Amys were not watching *Days of Our Lives,* because Mel Eng—an "Amy" and one of the three most heinous creatures on the planet—was right here.

Grow up, Amy

M·a·k·i·n·g F·r·i·e·n·d·s

Grow up, Amy

Kate Andrews

This edition published in 2001.

Text copyright © 1997 by Dan Weiss Associates, Inc.

Published by Troll Communications L.L.C.

All rights reserved. No part of this book may be reproduced or utilized in any form or by any means, electronic or mechanical, including photocopying, recording, or by any information storage and retrieval system, without written permission from the publisher.

This paperback edition published in 2000.

First published in 1997 by Macmillan Children's Books.
Reprinted by arrangement with William Morrow & Company.

Photography by Jutta Klee.

Printed in Canada.

10 9 8 7 6 5 4 3

The Wicked Mother
Another tale of unspeakable horror
by Carrie Mersel
(Note to myself: Keep hidden from Mom)

Heather's eighteenth birthday was a day she would remember for the rest of her life.

The morning dawned bleak and rainy in the town of Stony Brook. Heather awoke with a sense of foreboding, her mood as dark as the gray sky. She didn't understand it. She was turning eighteen. She should have been happy.

There was a knock on her bedroom door.

"Who is it?" Heather asked.

"It's your mother," came the reply.

Heather didn't want to answer the door. In truth, she had always suspected there was something evil about her mother. All the signs pointed to wickedness: her strange disappearances at all hours of the day or night, the bizarre company she kept—and most obviously, her fascination with witchcraft.

"What do you want?" Heather asked.

"I have a little present for you. . . ."

One

Clackety-clack went the antique typewriter keys.

Carrie Mersel was on a roll. She could feel it. She'd been hunched over her battered oak desk for the past hour, typing like somebody who was possessed. It was too bad she wouldn't be able to enter *this* story in a fiction contest. This was going to be one of her best. Yup. No doubt about it.

Of course, it didn't hurt that the house was empty. She always wrote better when nobody was around. It was like heaven. No TVs were blaring. No computerized gizmos were beeping. And it had pretty much been like this since Sunday. Her mom had been tied up with lame social engagements all week.

Monday, her mom had gone to a computer exhibition in Seattle. Tuesday, she'd helped design a dorky web site about old TV shows. Wednesday, she'd taken her gourmet cooking class. And today, Elizabeth Mersel was becoming an official member of some other weird club—her fourth. Carrie couldn't even remember what it was.

Not that it mattered. The only thing that mattered was that her mother was out of the house.

Silence, Carrie said to herself. Once again, her fingers flew over the keyboard. Why did her parents even bother living here anymore? She was the only one who spent any time at home. She should just demolish this house and build another right in its place. One with big, thick stone walls and dark stained-glass windows. One that wasn't swimming in the heinous colors of peach and white.

"Hello, dear!"

Who the—?

Carrie nearly fell off her chair.

Her mom was standing in the doorway with a wide smile on her face.

"Mom!" Carrie gasped. She forced a weak grin. "You scared me. I didn't even hear you come in."

"Sorry, honey!" Mrs. Mersel sang out. She flipped on the light and marched over to Carrie's window. Her cream-colored linen pants swished and swooshed as she moved. She tossed her long blonde hair over her shoulder, then tugged open Carrie's black velvet drapes, flooding the bedroom with afternoon sunlight.

Carrie blinked a few times.

"Uh . . . Mom?" she asked. "Do you really think we need to turn on the light *and* open the curtains?"

Mrs. Mersel sighed. "Carrie, one of these days, you're really going to hurt those beautiful hazel eyes of yours, you know that? You sit up here in the dark, squinting at that heap of junk on your desk—"

"Okay, okay," Carrie interrupted. She was definitely not in the mood to argue—especially about her typewriter. "So what are you doing home? I thought you had some meeting with a new club or something."

Her mom's perky smile abruptly reappeared. "I did!" she cried. She sat on the edge of Carrie's bed. "Today was more of a get-to-know-you type of thing than an actual meeting. But, Carrie, it was so*oo* much fun."

I'll bet, Carrie thought. "What's the club again?"

"The Ocean's Edge Garden Club," Mrs. Mersel answered proudly.

"Oh." Carrie nodded, trying not to laugh. Her mom wasn't exactly the outdoorsy type. As far as Carrie knew, her mother didn't even own a pair of sneakers—much less any gardening tools.

"But here's the thing I just *have* to tell you," Mrs. Mersel babbled excitedly. "I met the most interesting woman there. And guess what? She has a daughter your age!"

Oh, no. Carrie started shaking her head. *No, you don't. . . .*

"Anyway, this woman has had a fascinating life," her mom went on. "She moved here from China in the mid-seventies, and she speaks five languages, and she loves . . ."

Carrie didn't even bother to listen. She knew exactly where this was heading. She was going to have to meet some lame, spoiled brat who was "her age." Her mother seemed to think that if she stuck Carrie in a room with any girl whose mom knew Carrie's mom, the two girls would become lifelong soul mates.

". . . So they'll be here tomorrow at four for tea. Isn't that great?"

Carrie's eyes widened. Tomorrow was Friday. And this Friday, she was supposed to be on Skyler Foley's boat with the rest of her friends, sailing around the peninsula—far away from here.

"Wait . . . did you say tomorrow?" she asked.

Her mom nodded enthusiastically.

"Mom—I can't be here tomorrow," Carrie protested. "I have plans."

Mrs. Mersel kept right on smiling. "Whatever they are, dear, I'm sure you can change them. This woman is going out of her way to bring her daughter—"

"Why did you just assume I'd be here?" Carrie interrupted. "I mean, shouldn't you have checked with me first? That is the polite thing to do, right?"

"Carrie, I don't ask very much of you," Mrs. Mersel stated. Her smile soured a little. "What are these plans, exactly?"

"Sky's parents are sailing their boat around the peninsula," Carrie explained. "They're going to have a cookout for all of us. Everybody's gonna be there and—"

"Carrie, *please*." Her mother laughed. "You can go on Skyler's boat anytime. This is an opportunity for you to do something new. Honestly, dear, you need to branch out a little. You spend all your free time with the same old crowd."

"So what?" Carrie cried. Now she was really offended. "They're my friends, Mom. You like them, too. At least I thought you did."

"Of course I like them, dear," her mother said gently. "That's not the issue here. I'm just saying that it's important to have new experiences and meet new people."

Carrie shook her head. "No, you're saying that I don't have a choice," she muttered.

Mrs. Mersel laughed again. "I suppose I am." She stood. "But in any case, you *will* be here tomorrow at four. Understood?"

Carrie turned and faced her typewriter. She understood, all right. She was just too depressed to answer. It was really pretty amazing. In less than five minutes, her good mood had been totally destroyed.

"Oh—and Carrie, do me a favor, won't you?" Mrs. Mersel said, pausing in the doorway. "Try to wear something pretty—something other than black. Okay?"

The door closed behind her.

Carrie laughed. Good old Mom. Sure. Carrie would try not to wear black. She just didn't know if she would try hard enough.

Her eyes flashed over the page sticking out of her typewriter. She wasn't sure if she could start writing again. Her concentration was totally shot. She wasn't very inspired, either—even though she couldn't help but notice how her mom's little visit sort of mirrored what was on the paper. Well, except for the part about witchcraft. But, hey, maybe that would be her mother's next club.

Yup. It was kind of a drag when real life imitated what happened in a made-up horror story. In fact, it totally stank.

Oh, well. Carrie just hoped this girl—whoever she was—would be at least semitolerable.

That wasn't too much to ask, was it?

Melissa Eng

Dear Diary,

I don't believe it. For like the billionth time, Mom has decided to play social director with my life.

My life. Not hers. My is the key word. My Friday afternoon. My time. It's not like I force her to hang out with my friends' moms, right? So why does she force me to hang out with her friends' lame daughters?

I bet she thinks that I don't have enough friends. That's the only possible explanation. She thinks I'm unpopular. Me. It's such a joke. Mom obviously has no idea what "popularity" means. She doesn't understand that popularity has nothing to do with the number of people you hang out with.

Look at me: I only hang out with two other people on a regular basis, and I'm one of the most popular girls at school. I'm not patting myself on the back or anything. It's true. Why should I lie? Everybody knows that The Amys rule Robert Lowell Middle School. Ask anybody, and they'll say that the three most popular girls in school are Amy Anderson, Aimee Stewart, and me.

But Mom doesn't get it. She thinks that I'm lonely. That's why she makes me hang out with all these dorky kids. The pathetic thing is that <u>she's</u> the lonely one. The only reason she joins those stupid clubs—like the Ocean's Edge Garden Club, for example—is to hang out with as many different people as possible.

But it's her life, right? I don't interfere. Whatever makes her happy is cool.

So why does she interfere with me? I don't <u>need</u> any more friends. Amy and Aimee are the two greatest friends anyone could have. They're enough. They're <u>more</u> than enough.

All the complaining in the

world won't do a bit of good,
though. It's not like I have a
choice. My Friday is going to be
ruined. I'm going to spend it
with some girl I don't even know,
at some place I've never been,
talking about stupid stuff. . . .

  Blech. It's beyond depressing. I
just know that this girl is going to
be a dork. I just know it.

Two

I

"Why would your mom do something like that?" Amy asked.

"I don't know," Mel groaned.

"She knows that we watch our tape of *Days of Our Lives* at four," Aimee mumbled. "It doesn't make any sense."

Mel just shrugged. Aimee was right. It didn't make sense—but there was nothing she could do about it now. Mel's mom didn't understand the importance of *Days of Our Lives*. And in half an hour, Mel would be introducing herself to some loser while Aimee and Amy opened a fresh bag of Orange Milanos and tuned in to the latest episode.

"Let's go over to the corner," Amy said. "It's way too crowded here."

Mel nodded, following Amy as she pushed her way through the crowd on the front steps of Robert Lowell. Everybody seemed much too happy. Of course, it was Friday. School was over. But they didn't have to scream about it, did they?

Amy walked quickly, brushing her long blonde

hair behind one delicate ear. "Do you know anything at all about this girl?" she asked abruptly.

Mel shook her head. "I don't even know her name or where she lives."

"Maybe she'll be cool," Amy said. "Maybe—"

"There's your mom!" Aimee cried.

Mel looked up. Sure enough, Mrs. Anderson's gray Jaguar was pulling up to the curb. Aimee and Amy broke into a run. Mel was absolutely miserable. She almost felt as if they were running away from her. But who could blame them? She wasn't much fun to be around right now.

"Bye, Mel!" they both called at the same time.

The car doors slammed.

Mel frowned.

All right—just cheer up, she told herself. *It's only one afternoon of your life.*

Maybe Amy was right. Maybe this girl would be cool.

Yeah, right. And maybe Brick the bus driver would win the Mr. Universe contest.

II

"Are you sure you can't come with us?" Sky asked Carrie as the bus roared away from the school building. "Why don't you just skip the whole thing and make up an excuse later?"

Carrie hung her head. "Because my mom would kill me," she mumbled. "She has it all planned out.

I'm supposed to become best friends with this girl by six o'clock tonight."

Sky smiled sympathetically, but Carrie couldn't smile back. It was hard enough for her to be crammed into the long backseat with Alex, Jordan, Sky, and Sam, knowing that they were all about to whoop it up on a sunset cruise while she was going to be stuck at home drinking tea with some preppy princess. Carrie glanced out the window. The day had to be perfect, didn't it? The evergreen trees were tinted with that beautiful autumn afternoon light, the kind of slanting sun that only came around at this time of year at this time of day.

"Maybe you could pretend you were kidnapped," Alex suggested. Her hopeful blue eyes peered at Carrie from under the bill of her green Sonics cap. "You could say that some guys grabbed you after school and tied you to a chair, but you managed to escape by chewing your way through the ropes."

Carrie laughed. "Yeah," she said dryly. "The kidnapping rope-chewing excuse always works."

"Hey, it's not like you're going to be missing a gourmet feast or anything," Jordan said, leaning across Sky. "I mean, look at it this way. The Foleys' idea of a cookout is serving up cold celery sticks and vegetarian tofu burgers. No offense, Sky."

Carrie didn't trust herself to speak. She knew Jordan was just trying to make her feel better. But it wasn't working.

The bus slowed to a stop in front of Sky's dock. Carrie peered out the window at the houseboat. Sky's parents were running around the front deck, setting up the grill and putting lawn chairs out. A little moan escaped Carrie's lips.

"Don't have too much fun," she murmured.

Sky glanced over her shoulder as the four of them headed for the door. "Hey—maybe you'll really like this girl," she said enthusiastically.

"Maybe you're right," Carrie replied. "Maybe we'll become great buddies and room together in college and have a big double wedding and our kids will get married."

Sky shrugged. "You never know. . . ."

III

"You look so pretty, Melissa," Mrs. Eng said in her slightly accented, commanding voice.

"Thanks," Mel mumbled. She glanced at herself in the rearview mirror as her mom parked on Whidbey Road. She didn't feel pretty. Her lips were curved downward and her black eyes were lifeless. She was wearing one of her favorite dresses, though—a hip-looking purple sheath she had borrowed from Amy. Why she had wasted it on a day like today, though, she had no clue.

"Isn't this a beautiful home?" her mom exclaimed as she turned the car engine off.

Mel squinted up the long driveway at the modern

white house with big glass windows. Something about this house was very familiar. Of course, it was right around the corner from Amy's place. . . .

"What's wrong?" Mrs. Eng asked.

"Uh, nothing," Mel said uncertainly. "It's just . . . I didn't know your friend lived in Taylor Haven."

Mrs. Eng nodded happily, clutching her shiny purse with both hands. "You know—I wouldn't be surprised if this girl went to Robert Lowell."

Neither would I, Mel thought.

She *did* know this house. The bus stopped here every morning. But she couldn't place who lived here. Of course, knowing the people who rode Bus #4, the possibilities were all pretty weak. This was going to be a long afternoon.

IV

Carrie's eyes roved over all the empty seats as the bus climbed Pike's Way. There were only five other kids on the bus besides her. Well, of course: It was Friday. Everybody else was going somewhere fun. Whatever their idea of fun was. She knew at least three of the regular passengers were doing something totally lame—namely, The Amys. They were about to watch *Days of Our Lives.*

The bus turned and jerked to a quick stop in front of Carrie's driveway.

Party time, Carrie groaned to herself.

"Why the long face?" Brick asked. He flashed

Carrie a crazed grin as she trudged past him. "It's the weekend, man! Time to let loose!"

"Not for me it isn't," she mumbled. "See ya later, Brick. Have fun."

"Always do, Carrie. Hey, cool threads, by the way." He closed the door behind her.

Carrie waved as the bus pulled away. She allowed herself a little smile as she walked up the driveway. Her mom wouldn't think these clothes were so cool. Carrie had deliberately chosen the blackest possible outfit: a black skirt and black T-shirt, with her favorite black sweater to cap it off—the one with the black metal buttons. And, of course, she'd gone with black nail polish and combat boots to complete the look.

Perfect for meeting her future best friend, right?

"Carrie!" her mom called from the front door. "Come on, honey. The guests are already here."

"You want me to leap for joy?" Carrie muttered under her breath.

"Carrie, I told you not to wear black today," Mrs. Mersel hissed in a low whisper. "Melissa is dressed so nicely—"

"Good for her, Mom," Carrie said, stepping into the hallway. She mustered up the biggest smile she could, then turned to face the two people sitting on the lone peach-colored couch in the living room. "Hi—"

She froze, and her jaw dropped.

No, she thought, utterly horrified. *Not her . . .*

Well, well, well.

One thing was for sure. Carrie would not become lifelong friends with this girl. There would be no college rooming or double wedding.

She could rule out something else, too: All of The Amys were not watching *Days of Our Lives*, because Mel Eng—an "Amy" and one of the three most heinous creatures on the planet—was right here.

Three

For a long while, Carrie couldn't move. She couldn't even speak. She could only stare unbelievingly at the two people standing in her living room.

"I knew it," Mel started muttering. She hung her head. Her black pigtails drooped over her shoulders. "I knew something like this would happen."

"So you two girls know each other!" Mrs. Mersel exclaimed. She marched across the front hall toward the living room. Her heels clattered on the marble floor. "That's wonderful!"

Carrie started laughing. Wonderful? No—but she could think of a few other choice words.

"Don't just stand there, Carrie," her mother scolded. "Come here and introduce yourself to Mrs. Eng."

This must be some sort of bad karma or something, Carrie thought. She forced herself to walk toward Mel and Mrs. Eng. *Horrible things like this don't happen unless there's a reason. Did I do something bad? If I did, I'm sorry. I'm so very, very sorry. . . .*

"It's lovely to meet you, Carrie," Mrs. Eng said sincerely. She gathered herself up off the couch and extended a perfectly manicured hand.

Carrie shook it as politely as she could manage. "Nice to meet you, too, Mrs. Eng," she replied. She cast a sidelong glance at Mel, who was very deliberately avoiding Carrie's eyes by staring at the floor.

"Hello, Carrie," Mel groaned. She didn't look up.

"Melissa—is that any way to greet your hostess?" Mrs. Eng hissed.

Carrie smiled. After only three seconds, she could tell that Mrs. Eng and her mom were a perfect match. They were both really formal, they wore the same kinds of expensive designer business suits, and they both liked to embarrass their kids in front of other people.

"Melissa?" Mrs. Eng prodded.

Mel rolled her eyes. "Fine," she muttered. She pushed herself to her feet and faced Carrie with a phony grin. "Carrie, it's so nice to see you for, like, the eightieth time today," she said in a flat voice.

"Speak for yourself," Carrie answered sweetly.

"Carrie!" Mrs. Mersel barked. But then she let out a nervous little laugh. "Uh . . . why don't you pull up a chair?"

"Good idea," Carrie mumbled. That would kill a nice ten seconds or so—anything to delay an actual conversation with the Engs. She walked to the far wall as slowly as she could, picked up a hard-backed white chair, then lazily pushed it across the thick rug to the couch.

Tick, tick, tick went the clock.

"We were just talking about computers," Mrs. Eng said.

Perfect, Carrie thought. This really was bad karma. Not only did she hate computers, she'd even given her laptop to Sam. And her mom still didn't know anything about it.

"We can always talk about something else, though," Mel muttered.

Carrie slid onto her chair. "Sounds good to me," she agreed.

"Oh, isn't this funny!" Mrs. Mersel chirped. She squeezed in beside Mel's mom on the couch. "Carrie, you and Mel have something in common. You both have this strange phobia when it comes to—"

"Mom, *please*," Carrie interrupted. She forced another smile. "Didn't our guest say she wanted to talk about something else?"

"Listen, I don't have any phobia or anything," Mel muttered. "It's just that there are about a million other things to talk about that are about a million times more interesting than—"

"Melissa, please, you're being impolite," Mrs. Eng whispered sternly. "Enough."

"Oh, that's all right," Mrs. Mersel said with a breezy laugh. "Carrie always gets a little testy when we try to talk about anything computer-related. That might be something else you two girls have in common."

Carrie's smile vanished. Testy? Something they

had in common? That was it. She'd already had way more of this lame gathering than she could take.

"You know what else we have in common?" Carrie grumbled under her breath. "Neither of us wants to be in this living room with you two right now."

Mrs. Mersel's eyes narrowed. "Carrie, there's no need—"

"Why don't Carrie and I go to Carrie's room?" Mel suddenly suggested. "You two can talk about what you want to talk about, and we can talk about what we want to talk about."

There was another awkward silence. Carrie shot a quick glance at Mel. That wasn't a bad idea. If they were alone, they wouldn't have to be polite to each other. They wouldn't have to do anything. They wouldn't even have to speak to each other. Besides, anything was better than being stuck in here with her mom.

"You know, I think that's a great idea," Carrie proclaimed, hopping to her feet.

"I bet you two want to talk about the garden club, right?" Mel added. "That really wouldn't interest us. We'll just be in Carrie's room."

Mrs. Eng and Carrie's mother exchanged bewildered glances.

"Bye!" Carrie called. She abruptly turned and marched for the stairs.

Mel followed close on her heels.

No, this isn't a bad idea at all, Carrie said to herself.

Being alone with Mel was much better than hanging out with their mothers.

Besides, there was always a chance that she and Mel would be friendly, right?

There was an even better chance that she would ignore Mel completely.

Four

Black velvet drapes, Mel said to herself. *It figures. How cheesy can you get?*

Carrie slammed her door behind the two of them. Mel took a look around the room and shook her head. She should have known what it would be like. It was totally dark and depressing. The walls were covered with posters of lame grunge rock bands she'd never heard of. Everybody looked really pale and unhealthy and angry—as if they hadn't slept in weeks and were really mad about it.

"Nice room," Mel muttered sarcastically.

Carrie didn't answer. She sat down at her beaten-up old desk and immediately began poking at her typewriter.

Mel folded her arms across her chest. "Uh . . . hello?" she said, clearing her throat.

"What?" Carrie asked. She didn't even bother turning around.

"Sorry—but what am I supposed to do while you sit there and type?" Mel demanded.

Carrie shrugged her shoulders. "Do whatever you want," she muttered. "Read a book or something."

Mel raised her eyebrows. "A book?" She didn't even want to think about the kind of books Carrie Mersel read.

"Look, Mel—I don't want to talk to you and you don't want to talk to me," Carrie stated. "That's why we came up here, right? So we wouldn't have to talk to each other?"

Mel said nothing. Carrie was right, obviously. But she still hadn't expected her to pretend as if she, Mel, weren't even here. It was so insulting.

"Make yourself at home," Carrie mumbled over the clacking of the typewriter keys. "Just don't turn on the light and don't open the shades."

Mel pursed her lips. *Why?* she wondered. *Because vampires melt in the sunlight?* But she kept her mouth shut. Carrie was right: Neither of them wanted to talk. With a loud sigh, she sat down on the edge of Carrie's unmade bed. Her eyes roved across the room. They came to rest on a stack of bookshelves near Carrie's night table.

Now here was something shocking.

Carrie Mersel actually had some halfway decent books.

Mel slid across the bed and peered at the top shelf closely. There were about thirty different books by Stephen King. She couldn't believe it. She'd always thought that she had a lot of Stephen King books. But this was ridiculous. She'd never even heard of most of them.

"The Shining!" she heard herself exclaiming out loud.

The typing stopped abruptly.

"What about it?" Carrie asked, sounding bored.

"Uh . . . nothing." Mel glanced over her shoulder. That was embarrassing. Could she have sounded like more of a geek?

"Have you read it?" Carrie asked.

"No," Mel mumbled. "I've wanted to read it ever since my parents rented the movie, but I've never gotten around to buying it."

"Oh." Carrie hunched back over the typewriter. "Well, the movie is totally different."

"A lot of Stephen King movies are," Mel said absently.

Carrie swiveled around in her chair. "Wait a second," she said. "Are you trying to tell me you like Stephen King?"

"Yeah," Mel replied. She knew she sounded defensive, but she couldn't help it. "So?"

"No—it's . . . uh, nothing." Carrie laughed softly. "I'm just kind of surprised."

Mel rolled her eyes. "Carrie—you're not the only one who reads, you know. Tons of people like Stephen King. He's sold, like, forty zillion books."

Carrie shrugged. "I know. I guess I'm surprised because none of my friends like him."

"Well, none of my friends do, either," Mel shot back.

For a moment, their eyes locked.

Oh no, Mel thought. *Why did I say that? Mrs. Mersel was right. I do* have *something in common with Carrie.*

I should never have opened my big mouth. . . .

Carrie grinned. "So which one is your favorite?" she asked.

"I don't like him all that much," Mel lied, clumsily turning back to the bookshelf. She didn't want Carrie to get any crazy ideas—like they had some kind of bond now or something. "I don't really have a favorite." Then her voice fell to a low murmur. "Well, I kind of like *Carrie* . . . I mean, if I had to choose."

"What a coincidence," Carrie said dryly. "Me too."

Mel frowned. Carrie wasn't making fun of her, was she? She glanced over her shoulder.

But Carrie was still grinning. She raised her eyebrows. "I mean, it's kind of obvious, isn't it?"

Mel's brow grew furrowed. "What is?"

"*Duh*," Carrie said. "It's my name, Mel."

"Oh, right." Mel's face grew flushed and she quickly turned away again. That *was* kind of obvious. Now Carrie probably thought she was an airhead. Great. And knowing how much of a smart aleck Carrie was, she would probably make some wise comment. . . .

"You can borrow *The Shining* if you want," Carrie said casually.

Mel hesitated.

"Or you can pay eight dollars for it in some overpriced bookstore," Carrie muttered. She started typing again.

"Maybe I will borrow it," Mel said after a moment. She reached forward and pulled the battered paperback off the bookshelf. "Is it really okay?" she asked suspiciously.

"Sure," Carrie replied. She laughed. "I mean, I know where to find you—"

There was a loud knock on the door.

Mel whirled around.

"Carrie, that's not your typewriter I hear, is it?" Mrs. Mersel's muffled voice demanded.

Before Carrie could even answer, the door flew open.

"Mom!" she protested.

Mrs. Mersel stood in the doorway, shaking her head. "You're typing while you have company," she said in a tight voice. "You really have no manners at all, young lady." She glanced at Mel. "I'm sorry, dear. You'll have to excuse my daughter's rudeness."

Mel swallowed. She actually felt kind of bad for Carrie. It *was* sort of rude for her to sit there and type, but still . . .

"It's okay, Mrs. Mersel," she heard herself saying. She held up the book. "I was reading. We were just hanging out, doing our own thing."

All at once, a big smile broke out on Mrs. Mersel's face. "Really?" she asked.

Mel nodded.

"Well, excuse me," she said, clasping her hands together. She was beaming now. "I'm sorry, Carrie. Look at you. This is just so nice. . . ."

Mrs. Eng's head appeared in the doorway. "How

are you two doing?" she asked happily.

Oh, please, Mel grumbled to herself.

"They're like two peas in a pod," Mrs. Mersel chirped. "It's wonderful. They're already at the comfortable silence stage."

Mel's eyes widened. Comfortable silence stage? The woman had to be kidding.

Carrie started shaking her head. There was a sickly look on her face. "No," she choked out. "No, we're not—"

"What do you expect?" Mrs. Eng chuckled. "They're school chums."

"School chums!" Mel cried. Now that was ridiculous. "Give me a break, Mom!"

Mrs. Eng looked puzzled. "I don't understand. . . ."

Mel leaped off the bed and marched for the door. If she didn't understand, then Mel would just have to show her. Yes, things had gone far enough for one day. She and Carrie Mersel were not "chums"—and they never would be.

"What are you doing?" Mrs. Eng hissed as Mel brushed passed her. "What's going on?"

"I'm leaving," Mel stated, gripping the book tightly at her side. She hurried down the stairs. "You can stay if you want," she called. "I'm outta here. Thanks, Mrs. Mersel!"

"Melissa!" her mom shouted. "Come back here—"

Mel slammed the front door behind her.

There, she said to herself.

Then she realized something unpleasant.

She couldn't go anywhere. She was stuck. After all, she needed a ride home, didn't she?

What did I just do?

That had been a really, really dumb move. She'd shown her mom, all right—but she knew right then that storming out wouldn't do a bit of good. Her mom was obviously going to punish her for being so rude.

Mel could just guess what that punishment would be, too.

She was going to have to do something incredibly lame—like apologize formally to Carrie Mersel.

Or even worse, she was going to have to come back here and spend another afternoon with Carrie all over again.

Saturday:

The Morning After . . .

EARLY MORNING
THE ENG HOUSE

Mrs. Eng calls Mrs. Mersel. She apologizes once again for Mel's rude behavior and suggests that the four of them get together Monday afternoon. Mrs. Mersel gladly accepts.

MIDMORNING
THE MERSEL HOUSE

Mrs. Mersel informs Carrie that she'll be spending another afternoon with the Engs this Monday. And no—Carrie doesn't have a choice. After all, Carrie must have given Mel a reason for storming out, right?

LATE MORNING
THE ENG HOUSE

Mel receives a call from Amy. Amy's mom is taking the three of them to the movies on Monday afternoon. No, she isn't. She's taking two of them. Mel will be spending yet another afternoon with Carrie Mersel. Yes, *the* Carrie Mersel. She'll explain later. She's way too bummed out right now.

NOON
THE MERSEL HOUSE

Carrie receives a call from Alex. Can she come over to her house after school on Monday? Carrie tells Alex the terrible truth: She has to hang out with Mel Eng. That's right—*Mel Eng*. She'll explain later. She's way too bummed out right now.

Five

I

"So what's Carrie's house like?" Amy whispered the moment Mel sat down for lunch. Her bright blue eyes sparkled. "Is it totally freakish?"

"Yeah," Aimee said eagerly. "Does it smell or anything?"

Mel hung her head, staring into her bowl of chili. Usually she looked forward to lunch on Mondays. She looked forward to sitting at their little table and going over all the juicy weekend gossip. She looked forward to planning a bunch of good stuff for the week ahead. But today, naturally, she was going to spend the entire lunch answering a lot of embarrassing questions about her stupid afternoon with Robert Lowell's biggest weirdo.

"You guys?" she mumbled. "Can we talk about something else? It's depressing enough as it is. I mean, I actually have to go back there this afternoon."

Amy shook her head and laughed. "Just answer the question, Mel."

"Yeah, come on, Mel," Aimee pleaded. "I'm

curious. Something strange must go on in that house."

Mel grinned slightly in spite of herself. "Well, it doesn't smell or anything," she muttered. "But her room is kind of a scary place."

The two of them shoved their trays aside and leaned forward. "Yeah?" they whispered at precisely the same time.

Mel glanced at her girlfriends. Her grin widened. Maybe talking about her stupid afternoon wasn't so bad. They were hanging on her every word.

"Well, for starters, when I went in there, I could barely see a thing," Mel whispered. "She has these totally tacky black velvet drapes—"

"Black velvet?" Amy hissed, making a face.

Mel nodded. "Yeah. But get this. They completely cover her windows. No sun can get in at all. And she *freaked* when I asked if I could turn the light on."

II

"So, anyway, Mel comes into my room," Carrie said. "And she's all like, 'Hel-*lo*. What am I supposed to be doing while you sit there and amuse yourself?'"

Carrie took a deep breath. She felt as if she'd been ranting and raving about Mel Eng for hours now. But she couldn't stop. Everyone at the table was obviously way into this story. Jordan was laughing. Alex was shaking her head. Sky looked horrified, as if she had witnessed the whole thing herself. They hadn't touched their lunches. Even Sam—the boy who hated getting involved in other people's problems—was gazing at her with wide black eyes.

This was actually kind of fun.

"What did you tell her?" Sky asked.

Carrie shrugged. "I was like, 'Read a book. Do whatever you want. Make yourself at home.' You know, just to be polite. There was no point in making a bad situation worse."

"And?" Alex prodded.

"And she was totally rude, of course," Carrie replied. "She was all like, 'I don't want to read any of your stupid books.' But then she saw one that she wanted, and she started making this huge deal about how she'd never read it. You know—she was obviously hinting that I should give it to her or something."

Carrie was beginning to realize something as she jabbered away. Her story had very little to do with what really happened.

At first, she was planning on exaggerating only a teeny little bit—just for dramatic effect, of course. Every good story had to have some exaggeration. It wasn't as though she wanted to lie or anything. But the more she got into it, the more she got carried away. She couldn't help herself. Besides, she was entertaining her friends, right? That was what counted.

"Did you give her the book?" Sam asked.

"Of course," Carrie said evenly. "I had to do something to shut her up."

III

"And that was when things got really out of control," Mel whispered.

Amy and Aimee leaned even closer.

"So Carrie was typing this whole time, right?" she continued. "She was acting like a total freakazoid and completely ignoring me. I felt like I was in a room with a psycho or something."

Amy raised her eyebrows. "You were, Mel," she stated.

Mel laughed. She was having a blast. It was unbelievable. The three of them were hunched together so closely now that their foreheads were practically touching. She'd never been the center of attention like this. Then again, it was kind of hard to be the center of attention when your best friend was Amy Anderson. Amy wasn't the type of person who enjoyed sharing the spotlight all that much.

"So I reach for a book on Carrie's bookshelf," Mel breathed. "Just to kill some time. She has, like, a billion books—all by these weird people I've never even heard of. And just as I pull down a book, she spins around and totally wigs out on me. She was like, 'What are you doing with that? Don't touch my stuff!' And I'm like, 'Excuse *me*. I'm not trying to

41

steal your books or anything. Just chill.'"

Amy leaned back and shook her head. "You know, Mel, I'm not surprised," she commented in a very serious voice. Her eyes darted over toward Carrie's table. "Carrie's insane. Really."

Mel hesitated. "Insane?"

"That's right," Amy said.

"Really?" Aimee asked excitedly.

"Really." Amy nodded. "I'm not joking. She's got a split-personality disorder or something. Remember that time she invited herself over to my house and wigged out on me? There was no reason for it. It was like she suddenly became a different person. I bet she's taking medication."

Mel didn't say anything. For the briefest instant, she felt the tiniest pang of something uncomfortable. It wasn't guilt, exactly. She *was* pretty much making stuff up as she went along—not that it mattered. Carrie was a dork. Still, she kind of doubted if Carrie was really, truly insane or anything. . . .

"If she's crazy, maybe that's why she wears all black all the time," Aimee mumbled.

Mel managed an awkward smile. "Maybe."

"So go on," Amy prompted. "What else?"

IV

Carrie lowered her voice to a whisper. She couldn't tell if The Amys were trying to listen in on her conversation—but judging from the way the three of them kept sneaking peeks in her direction, it was probably safe to assume the worst.

"Suddenly, my mom and Mel's mom literally burst into my room," she murmured. "And they see Mel sitting there with a book and me at the typewriter . . . and you'll never guess what my mom said."

She bit her lip, glancing around the table. Everyone's face was glazed with a totally rapt expression. Nobody said a word.

Carrie took a deep breath. "She said, 'Isn't this wonderful! Carrie and Mel are already at the comfortable silence stage!'"

Jordan started cracking up. "Come on, Carrie—"

"Shh!" Carrie whispered, but she was laughing, too. It figured that Jordan wouldn't believe the only true part of the story. "I swear, that's what she said. But that's not all. Because after she said it, Mel went off. I mean she flipped. She started yelling at her mom and then she stomped out of the house and slammed the door."

Sky's mouth fell open. "Really? Mel always seems so calm and collected—"

"Believe me, she isn't," Carrie muttered. That much was true, too, at least. Well, she thought it was. Mel *had* thrown a huge temper tantrum. But Carrie had been adding so many little details that it was getting harder to remember what really had happened and what hadn't.

"I don't get why your mom is making you hang

out with her again this afternoon," Alex said. "It's crazy."

Carrie shrugged. "Yeah, but my mom isn't known for being sane."

"So, what do you think is gonna happen?" Sky asked anxiously.

"Who knows?" Carrie sighed. "But I'm looking at it this way. It can't get much worse than what happened on Friday."

Six

Mel couldn't bring herself to get out of her seat.

Everyone was waiting. The bus door was open. The engine was quietly humming. She could hear birds chirping in the trees in front of Carrie's house. But she couldn't move.

This is the most humiliating moment of my life.

Coming back here was bad enough. But somehow, knowing that every single kid on Bus #4 was watching her . . . *Blecch.* She could just predict what would happen. Some loser was going to tell some other loser that Mel Eng—one of The Amys, one of the rulers of Robert Lowell—had gone to Carrie Mersel's house Monday afternoon. And by tomorrow, the entire student body would be convinced that Mel Eng and Carrie Mersel were best friends.

"Come on, Mel," Carrie muttered under her breath as she hurried out the door. "Move it."

"Yeah, Mel," Aimee teased loudly. She gave Mel a hard nudge with her elbow. "Your new best buddy is waiting for you."

Mel frowned. "Very funny," she growled. She lumbered to her feet.

"You're getting off here?" Brick exclaimed. "Wow. I didn't even know that you guys hung out together. I must really be out of it."

Amy and Aimee started giggling.

Mel shook her head. *Thanks, Brick.* That guy never had a thought that he didn't actually say out loud.

"Have fun!" he called. The door squeaked shut behind her, and the bus roared down Whidbey Road—right past her mom's little blue BMW.

"Great," she moped.

"What?" Carrie asked.

"My mom is already here. That means she's gonna make a huge scene and make me apologize, like, a hundred times and—"

"Look, I don't want that any more than you do," Carrie interrupted. The two of them paused at the front door. Carrie lowered her voice. "A big scene will be totally embarrassing for both of us. So let's just say that you apologized at school, we made up, and that'll be that."

Mel thought for a second. It sounded good—but she doubted if that would work. Her mom always liked to make a big deal out of things. She brushed a few stray wisps of black hair away from her eyes. "Maybe . . ."

The door swung open.

"Hello, Melissa!" Mrs. Mersel cried happily. "I thought I heard you two whispering out there. Come in, come in."

Mel followed Carrie into the peach-and-white-checkered hallway and glanced into the living room. Her mom was standing by the couch, gazing at her sternly. So much for avoiding a scene.

"Hello, Melissa. Do you have something you want to say to Mrs. Mersel and Carrie before we all sit down?" Mrs. Eng asked.

Mel swallowed. She could tell her mom was mad. Her mom's accent was always more pronounced when she was upset about something.

"Sorry?" she murmured hopefully.

Mrs. Eng shook her head. "Mel, you need to do a little better than that."

"She's already said she's sorry to me, like, a million times," Carrie announced. "And I said I'm sorry to her. Everything's great. No hard feelings."

Mrs. Mersel tilted her head and smiled. "Well, that's fine, then. Apology accepted, Melissa."

A smile spread across Mel's face. That had been easy. Amazingly enough, Carrie had handled the situation pretty well.

"Well, I'd love to stay here and chat with all of you, but I have to study for a math test," Carrie said abruptly. She marched quickly up the stairs. "Mr. Engel announced a pop quiz for tomorrow, so . . ." Her voice trailed off.

Mel frowned. Now where did she think she was going?

"Carrie, you are *not* going to study for a math test

when we have company," Mrs. Mersel stated. She was still smiling, but her eyes had narrowed into two angry slits. "Put your backpack away and come back here."

Carrie paused at the top of the stairs and raised her hands apologetically. "I can't, Mom. You know how much trouble I have with math. You're always telling me how I need to study harder. I can't afford to mess this up. I need to get my priorities straight, right?"

Mel rolled her eyes. She'd never heard a bigger load of garbage in her life.

But Mrs. Mersel was no longer smiling. Her lips were pressed into a tight line.

"Carrie, Melissa might be able to help you," Mrs. Eng suggested from the living room. "Math is her strongest subject."

Jeez, Mom . . . Mel put her face in her hands. This was just what she needed. Her mom might as well have said, "Carrie, Melissa is a major geek. Tell the world tomorrow."

"Melissa?" her mom prodded. "You wouldn't mind, would you? You help your friend Amy with math all the time."

Mel's hands fell away from her face. "What does that have to do with anything?" she cried. "I help Amy because—"

"It has to do with thinking about someone besides yourself," Mrs. Eng cut in matter-of-factly.

"You know how grateful you are when someone helps you with your geography—"

"Fine," Mel grumbled. She was not going to get into a discussion about her geography problems in front of the Mersels. This whole situation was so ridiculous. If her mom only had the slightest clue, she would know that Carrie probably didn't even have a math quiz tomorrow. She was just making an excuse to avoid the whole get-together. Mel would have probably done the same thing if Carrie had come to her house.

"So, what do you say?" Mrs. Eng asked.

Mel shook her head. She glanced up at Carrie. "Do you really want me to help you with your math?" she asked, feeling like a fool.

Carrie stared at her blankly. "Whatever." She turned and disappeared up to the second floor.

"Melissa, you'll have to excuse Carrie's behavior," Mrs. Mersel murmured. "Math is a touchy subject around here. . . ."

"That's all right," Mel said, sighing. She moved slowly toward the stairs. It was weird: Her own mom had once said the same thing about geography—that it was a "touchy subject." Her mom and Carrie's mom were like long-lost twins. No wonder they were trying to force Mel and Carrie to be friends.

But today was going to be the last day she ever set foot in this house.

Yes, today Mel was going to have a little chat with

her mom. After all, if she spent any more time here, Carrie Mersel's weirdness might start rubbing off on her or something. . . .

And there was no way she was going to let that happen.

Seven

Why are they torturing me like this? Carrie wondered. She slouched down in front of her desk. She had been sure that the math quiz excuse would work. She was sure they would leave her alone. . . .

Mel sauntered into the room and closed the door without saying a word. She immediately spread herself out across Carrie's bed.

"Make yourself at home," Carrie mumbled sarcastically.

"Hey—I'm the one who's helping you study for your math quiz," Mel retorted.

Carrie turned to face her. "I don't have a math quiz, Mel."

"No kidding," she mumbled. She propped herself up against two oversized pillows, then carefully flattened the wrinkles in her designer bell-bottom jeans and sky blue baby-doll T-shirt. "Any normal person could have figured that out."

"So why did you come up?" Carrie asked.

"Because it's either stay in here with you or stay down there with them," Mel grumbled. "What would you do?"

Carrie didn't say anything. "I guess you have a point," she finally admitted.

Mel's eyes briefly flickered over Carrie's face. "Our moms . . . they're like . . ."

"'Like two peas in a pod!'" Carrie squealed in her mom's voice, adding the fake grin. She tossed her dyed black hair over her shoulders, imitating that irritating way her mom had of constantly fussing with her appearance.

Mel smirked. "Sure they are. They're garden club . . . *chums.*"

Carrie laughed. Their eyes met briefly. Then Mel blinked—and the next instant, she was wearing the same aloof and annoyed expression she always wore. Carrie sighed. Of course. Mel was obviously way too cool to admit that she had a sense of humor or anything.

"It is kind of freaky about our moms, though, isn't it?" Carrie asked after a minute, almost to herself. "I mean, they met . . . what? Four days ago? And it's like they've known each other their entire lives. Maybe they were separated at birth or something."

Mel frowned.

Oh, brother, Carrie thought. Now Mel was probably going to get offended that Carrie was ragging on Mrs. Eng so much.

"What?" Carrie demanded.

"Nothing, nothing," Mel murmured. She went

back to straightening her pants. "It's just that I was thinking pretty much the same thing right before I came up here."

Carrie raised her eyebrows. "You were?"

A fleeting grin crossed Mel's face. "Yeah—when your mom said that math was a touchy subject with you. That's exactly what my mom says about geography. She actually makes me stay home on the weekends to study." She looked up. "Can you believe that?"

"My mother does the same thing to me!" Carrie exclaimed. "I had to sneak out of the house two weeks ago because my mom knew I had a math quiz."

"Well . . . math I can kind of understand," Mel said simply. "Everybody has to know math. We use it every day. But geography? I mean, what's the point? If I really need to know where Tasmania is, I can look at a map, right?"

Carrie snickered. "Come on, Mel. And if I really need to know the square root of one hundred eighty-nine, I can use a calculator, right?"

Much to Carrie's surprise, Mel actually laughed. "I guess you're right," she said. "I mean, when it comes right down to it, what's the point of even going to school?"

Carrie shrugged. "There *is* no point," she said dryly. "That's the great thing about modern society. You've got calculators, maps, dictionaries, encyclopedias, computers, satellites. . . ."

"You've got everything," Mel agreed. She laughed again—and this time, it actually sounded sort of nice. "You know, somebody should tell that to Principal Cashen."

"Really." Carrie laughed, too. "Somebody should go up to him and be like, 'Look, buddy, I don't need your lousy school. I don't even need to get out of bed to learn everything I need to know.'"

"Can you imagine?" Mel said. She put her hands behind her head and leaned back into the pillows. "Maybe I should do that. Then once I stopped going to school, I wouldn't have to take any more geography tests. Maybe Mom would finally stop bugging me." Her voice flattened. "Maybe I'd even have time to join the Ocean's Edge Garden Club and mingle with the rich ladies."

"And wouldn't that be wonderful?" Carrie cried.

Mel smiled. "Fabulous," she stated, mimicking her own mom's voice. She let out a long sigh and shook her head. "Other kids' parents aren't as whacked-out as ours, are they?"

"None that I've met," Carrie mumbled.

Mel rolled over on her side and glanced at Carrie's bookshelf. "That's one of the reasons I like Stephen King so much," she joked. "All the scary characters remind me of people in my own life. Namely, my mom."

Carrie's eyes widened. Whoa. How many times

had that same thought crossed *her* mind?

For a moment, she leaned back in her chair and stared at Mel, struck by the weirdness of what was happening in here. She was actually having a normal conversation with Mel Eng. No, not a normal conversation: an enjoyable conversation. The girl *did* have a sense of humor. She had a frighteningly large number of things in common with Carrie, too. Sure—she was stuck up; she was spoiled . . . but she wasn't all bad.

"Have you started *The Shining*?" Carrie asked tentatively.

Mel nodded. She swung her legs over the side of the bed and sat up, then patted her black hair. "I read the first thirty pages," she began. "It's really—"

"Carrie!" Mrs. Mersel called from downstairs.

Carrie rolled her eyes. "*What?*" she groaned.

"Are you studying?" Mrs. Mersel demanded.

Carrie glanced at Mel. They both started grinning. "Yeah, Mom," Carrie stated flatly.

"Melissa—are you helping her?" Mrs. Eng chimed in.

Mel didn't answer. Her eyes bored deeply into Carrie's. They seemed to be asking: *What now?*

Carrie chewed her lip thoughtfully. Hmm. That was kind of an important question. If their parents knew that the two of them were actually talking, then they might get the wrong idea. They might even think that Carrie and Mel wanted to do this again or something. And Carrie was not prepared to waste any more afternoons with Mel Eng—even if Mel was a Stephen King fan. No, it would be much better if their parents thought they weren't capable of getting along at all.

"I think we're fighting," Mel whispered conspiratorially. "Don't you?"

Carrie nodded, smirking. "My thoughts exactly," she mouthed.

"Melissa?" Mrs. Eng called again.

"She isn't helping me, Mrs. Eng," Carrie shouted back.

"That's not true," Mel cried, getting into the act. "Carrie's lying. She's not studying at all. She's sitting at her desk, ignoring me."

"Come off it!" Carrie yelled. She was smiling now. "You've been acting like a jerk."

Mel was smiling now, too. *"Me?"* she shrieked. "What about you—"

The door flew open.

Their smiles instantly vanished.

"What's going on in here?" Mrs. Mersel demanded, marching into the room. "Carrie—why aren't you studying?"

"I—I . . ." Carrie stammered, waving her hands dramatically.

Mel hopped off the bed. "I'm sorry, Mrs. Mersel," she said in a very cold and polite tone. "I think it would be best for all of us if I just left."

Mrs. Eng stepped through the doorway. "Melissa, what did I tell you about—"

"I'm sorry, Mom—but what do you want me to do?" Mel pleaded. "This isn't working out, okay? Can I please go home?"

Carrie's mom and Mrs. Eng exchanged glances.

Carrie held her breath.

"Maybe Mel should go home," Mrs. Mersel said slowly.

Carrie breathed a sigh of relief. *Thank you, Mom.*

"And she can come back some other time," Mrs. Mersel finished.

Carrie's eyes bulged. "What?" she gasped.

Mrs. Mersel fixed Carrie with a frozen smile. "Some time when you aren't studying."

Carrie shot a horrified look at Mel, whose own face was wilting. "B-B-But—"

"Yes," Mrs. Eng stated. "That is an excellent idea."

"Mom!" Mel barked. "How can—"

"That's enough, Mel," Mrs. Eng continued, cutting her off. "There's no reason at all that you should keep acting so childish."

Carrie's heart sank. They just didn't get it. They didn't see that the two of them would never—no, could never—be friends. And if Carrie had to spend any more afternoons away from Alex and Sky and Jordan and Sam . . . well, they might start getting the wrong idea about her and Mel. Carrie swallowed hard. They weren't already getting the wrong idea, were they? She could just picture her friends hanging out at Alex's house and having an awesome time, wondering what she and Mel were really doing. . . .

"Whatever your differences are," Mrs. Eng concluded, "I just know you'll work them out."

Mrs. Mersel smiled broadly. "I couldn't agree more," she said. "You know the old saying: These things take time."

Mel

Dear Diary,
  So . . . the nightmare continues.
Our moms are obviously in a
state of denial. And it's not like
Carrie and I haven't been trying
to make our moms understand
that the idea of us being best
friends is absurd. We tried
everything. Today we even staged a
major fight. But the garden club
wonder twins still seem to think
that it's only a matter of time
before we go skipping arm in
arm into the sunset together.
  It's so incredibly . . . I
don't know how to describe it.
I'm more frustrated than I've
ever been in my whole life. When
Carrie's mom said to us that
"these things take time" —baloney,
I wanted to _scream._
  At least I know now that Amy
was wrong. Carrie is definitely
not insane. I've had some

firsthand experience with real live insanity in the past few days—and compared to our moms, Carrie is the most normal person in the whole world.

But you know what? All kidding aside, I'm a little worried. The more I hang out with Carrie, the less time I have to hang out with my real friends. When Aimee made that stupid crack on the bus today about my new "best buddy," I didn't give it a second thought. But now I can't _stop_ thinking about it. What if she wasn't joking? What if Amy and Aimee think that Carrie's lameness really _is_ rubbing off on me?

No. I know that's not true. Deep down, I know that I'm probably wigging out for no reason. But still, these kinds of thoughts have a way of creeping up on you and taking over your whole brain. . . .

Maybe that's why I also feel guilty. Because something else

has been bothering me lately, too. And it's something I can't admit to anyone — least of all Amy and Aimee. If they ever found out, I'd die.

I know this sounds weird, but I'm starting to think that Carrie isn't all that lame.

Like, she's really funny — in her own weird way, obviously. And when we staged that huge fight today . . . it was kind of like we were in on this private joke that nobody else in the world could possibly understand. We were united against our moms, but it was more than that. It was like there was this secret agreement between us. We had to fight. That's because we can never be friends in this lifetime. Our real friends would think we were both crazy, and they'd probably ditch us.

And in this totally strange, bizarre way, pretending that we hate each other makes us sort of like each other. It gives us some

kind of connection or something.
Well. _That_ makes no sense at
all, does it? I guess I already
_am_ crazy. Then again, that
wouldn't surprise me. Like
mother, like daughter, right?

Eight

"Melissa . . . ?"

Mel shook her head. She was not going to answer. She was way too into *The Shining* right now to deal with her mom.

"Melissa? Are you up there?"

Mel doggedly clutched the book in front of her face. But she couldn't concentrate. Her mom's voice was like a needling, unscratchable itch. The whole reason she'd shut herself up in her room and buried herself in bed with this book was because she specifically wanted to escape from—

"Mel*issa!*"

"*What*, Mom?" Mel shouted, glaring at the closed door. She let the paperback fall to the pillow beside her. "I'm reading, okay?"

There was a pause.

"Oh." Her mom's voice suddenly sounded muted and faraway. "Never mind."

Mel sighed. She knew what that meant. It meant: *Get out of bed and come down here.* "What do you want?" she asked.

"No, don't worry—"

Thank goodness the phone started ringing.

"I'll get it!" Mel cried. That would provide a convenient excuse to ignore her mom for a few more minutes. She hopped out of bed, walked across her book-littered floor, and grabbed the phone off her desk. "Hello?"

"Hi. Is Mel there, please?"

Mel paused. It was a girl—but she couldn't place the voice. "This is Mel," she replied.

"Oh. Hey. It's Carrie."

Mel blinked. Carrie? A weird flutter passed through her stomach. Why was *she* calling? Hadn't they had enough of each other for one day?

"Is this a bad time?" Carrie asked in the silence.

"What do you want?" Mel whispered. She knew she sounded harsh, but she couldn't help it. She was a little mad—not to mention nervous. Carrie shouldn't have called. If her mom knew that the two of them were talking, she might get all sorts of crazy ideas. . . .

"Look—you're a math whiz, right?" Carrie asked, unfazed by Mel's rudeness.

Mel frowned. That was a strange question. "Why?" she asked.

"Because I wanted to ask you a question about my geometry homework," Carrie said matter-of-factly. "I really do need help. I should have used you today when I had the chance."

"Oh." So this wasn't a social call. For some bizarre reason, Mel felt sort of let down. But why? It was only Carrie Mersel. Besides, her friends called her with math questions all the time. Amy needed help with her homework almost every single night.

Carrie sighed. "Look, if you're really busy or something—"

"No, no," Mel interrupted.

"Are you sure?" Carrie asked.

"Yeah." Mel absently twirled the phone cord around her fingers. "Really. It's either help you with geometry or help my mom with some bogus chore, like rinsing out a hundred old mayonnaise jars for recycling."

Carrie chuckled. "You're on recycling detail, too, huh?"

"Don't get me started," Mel groaned. She eased herself down into her cushiony desk chair and shook her head. "That's the least of my problems."

"Do you take out the garbage?" Carrie asked.

Mel grinned slightly. "Let's just say that I'm the one who has to deal with all the foul substances in the Eng household."

"Me too. Whenever my dad finds something gross that was buried in the back of the fridge for years—you know, moldy cheese or something—my mom's like, 'Don't touch it, dear. Why do you think we have Carrie?'"

"Me too!" Mel said, laughing. "It's like my parents don't want to risk contamination, so they send me in to do all the hazardous stuff."

"Yeah, well, just wait till the garden club gets going full swing," Carrie muttered.

Mel stopped laughing. "What do you mean?"

"I bet we're gonna be forced to haul around sacks of horse manure," Carrie said. "They use that stuff for fertilizer, you know."

Mel grimaced. "You're kidding, right?"

"I wish I were." Carrie sighed. "You think it's bad right now. Come springtime, you and I are gonna be hanging out every single day. The only difference is that we're gonna be knee-deep in poop."

"Carrie, please . . . ," Mel protested, but she was giggling again. Even though Carrie was being disgusting, the whole thing was funny. The thought of the two of them standing side by side in piles of horse manure . . .

Mel was kind of surprised at herself. She never talked about really gross stuff like this. Of course, compared with Carrie, her friends were a little prudish. So was she, for that matter.

"I'm just hoping my mom is gonna forget about gardening by then," Carrie added. "It isn't nearly high-tech enough for her. Plus, she's a total clean freak. She hates getting dirty."

"Mine too," Mel said dryly. "But that's why they need us. They're gonna sit back and watch while we do all of their really dirty work—"

"I thought you were reading, Melissa."

Mel glanced up with a start.

Her mom was standing in the doorway. She looked less than pleased, to say the least. Mel hadn't even heard her come in. Then again, her mother wasn't in the general habit of knocking.

"Well, I just picked up the phone, Mom," Mel hissed impatiently, cupping her hand over the mouthpiece.

"I know." Mrs. Eng's eyebrows were tightly knit. "I can hear you chattering and laughing all the way downstairs." Then her face softened a little. "Look, just tell Amy you can talk to her tomorrow at school. I need you to help me with the garbage."

Mel smirked. Her mom had no idea that she was on the phone with Carrie. That was good. What was bad was that her mom really did want her to do something nasty.

"What's going on?" Carrie whispered at the other end of the phone.

Mrs. Eng stood in the door, waiting.

"I . . . uh, gotta go," Mel mumbled.

"Is your mom there?" Carrie asked.

Mel let out a deep breath. "Exactly."

"That's cool," Carrie said. "Look, uh—I'll just call someone else. I'll talk to you later."

"Bye," Mel murmured. She placed the phone down on the hook.

Mrs. Eng turned and headed back downstairs. "It won't take long," she called. "When you're done with the garbage, you can clean your room."

"Gee—thanks, Mom," Mel muttered sarcastically.

Nag, nag, nag. Her gaze swept the floor. Her room wasn't that messy. So there were bunches of books on the floor. And Mr. Bubbles, her stuffed monkey, had fallen off the bed . . . but that was about it. She wondered for a moment if Carrie's mother nagged her as much. Probably not. Carrie's room wasn't very disorganized. There wasn't a whole lot of junk in Carrie's room left over from the second grade, like there was in her's.

"Come on, Melissa," her mom called. "I'd like to finish this before midnight."

"In a minute." Mel shook her head. Maybe she should get rid of some of her model ponies and stuffed animals. If anyone besides Amy and Aimee ever found out she slept with a big fluffy monkey, her reputation as one of the hippest, coolest girls in the state of Washington would probably be shot. She could just imagine what Carrie would think.

Hold on, she said to herself angrily.

Why would she even care what Carrie thought? They weren't friends. Okay, talking to her on the phone was fun. But that was just because Mel didn't have to act a certain way around her. Carrie was just another loser. More importantly, she was one of Amy Anderson's worst enemies. And any enemy of Amy's was also an enemy of Mel's.

"Melissa!" her mom yelled.

"Coming!" Mel pushed herself to her feet and

determinedly marched out of the room. *I don't like Carrie Mersel*, she swore to herself. *I'm not becoming friends with her. . . .*

But even as she silently uttered the words, she had a horrible feeling that they weren't true.

Nine

When Carrie got off the bus in front of Sky's houseboat on Tuesday afternoon, it was like coming home after a long, lame vacation. Finally everything was right again. She was hanging out with Alex and Sky after school. It was pouring rain. Carrie was sure that life didn't get any better than this.

The three of them scampered down the narrow rain-slicked dock, holding their backpacks over their heads in a futile attempt to keep dry—the way they always did.

Yup. Life was back to normal.

"Whew," Sky said breathlessly, shutting the door behind them. She tossed her backpack on the floor, then shook her long, damp, curly brown hair—just like a wet puppy dog. Water splattered all over the place.

"Hey!" Alex cried.

"What's the big deal?" Sky rubbed her face with the sleeve of her brown sweater and grinned. "You're already wet."

Alex laughed. "Yeah, but I kind of want to start drying off. . . ."

All of a sudden, Carrie noticed something. Alex

was decked out in her usual tomboy garb—baggy black pants, a soaked black T-shirt, sneakers—but one vital piece of her wardrobe was missing. It was the green Sonics cap she had stolen from her older brother, Matt. She always wore that hat. But today, her shoulder-length brown hair was uncovered, dripping, and plastered to the sides of her head.

"Where's your hat?" Carrie asked.

Alex flashed her a puzzled glance. "I didn't tell you?"

Carrie shook her head.

"Oh, man . . . ," she groaned.

"What?" Carrie asked.

Alex sighed deeply. "It's at the bottom of the sound," she mumbled.

"The *sound?*" Carrie asked incredulously.

Alex looked at Sky—and the two of them started cracking up.

"What happened?" Carrie asked.

Alex took a deep breath. "It's all Jordan's fault," she complained, collapsing onto the brown sofa in the little main cabin.

"We should have never let him near the grill," Sky added, sitting beside her.

Carrie just stood there, feeling completely clueless. "What did he do?"

"It happened Friday—when you were stuck hanging out with Mel," Sky explained. "He had the spatula, right? See, he was cooking the burgers

71

because my dad doesn't even really know how to cook real burgers. . . ."

"And he started waving the spatula around," Alex continued. "You know, acting like a total goof, as usual."

"He kept saying something, too," Sky added distractedly. She started laughing again. "It was like a rap. Something about 'The chef is cookin' and the burger is smokin'—I'm the best grill man and I ain't jokin'.'"

Alex rolled her eyes. "Something dorky."

Carrie was smiling along with them, but the more they talked, the more she began to feel an odd sort of emptiness inside. Her smile became strained. Whatever Jordan had done had obviously been really funny, and she had totally missed out on it. And her friends had forgotten to tell her about it.

"So anyway," Alex went on, "Jordan starts flipping burgers. But he's out of control. Finally one goes over the side of the boat and *plop*—right into the water. Everybody starts yelling, but Jordan doesn't stop. The next one goes into the air. I make a dive for it. But Jordan does, too. With the spatula. So we go slamming into each other, and the spatula catches the bill of my hat . . . and, well, you can guess the rest. The hat sank like a stone when it hit the water. The burgers floated, but my hat sank." She giggled. "Can you believe that?"

Carrie just shrugged.

"It was totally amazing," Sky said. "It was like one of those slow-motion replays you see at a football game. The hat goes flying, and the burger goes flying, and these two things are, like, hanging in the air, and everybody is freaking out. . . ."

Carrie swallowed. She couldn't smile anymore. And she was angry, too, because she couldn't figure out why she was so upset. So she had missed something funny. Big deal. It wasn't as if Jordan's dumb antics had changed anybody's life in any major way. But she felt . . . outside somehow. She wasn't a part of this. And there was nothing she could do to become a part of it. She couldn't change the past.

"Hey, Carrie—are you all right?" Alex asked.

"Huh?" Carrie glanced at the two of them.

They were both staring at her with alarmed looks on their faces. She hadn't even noticed.

She shook her head, forcing herself to smile again. "Uh . . . yeah," she mumbled. "I was just thinking about how I'm going to have to hang out with Mel. Again."

Alex nodded thoughtfully. She scooted over into the middle of the couch and slapped the empty spot, moist now from her wet clothes.

Carrie sighed and slumped down beside her.

"You're really bummed, huh?" Alex murmured.

Carrie nodded. That was true—to some extent. She was bummed that she would have to miss another afternoon with Sky and Alex. Of course, she wasn't dreading this visit with Mel nearly as much as she had dreaded the last one.

"What happened yesterday, anyway?" Sky asked. "Did Mel throw another fit?"

Carrie hesitated for just a moment. Her eyes wandered out the window—through the rain to where Puget Sound met the sky in a seamless blur of dull gray. Once again, it was time to spin a tale about Mel. So why wasn't she psyched? Yesterday, she'd had the time of her life talking about Mel. But that was before last night's phone call and the fake fight.

"We got in a fight," she said finally.

"Lemme guess." Alex gave her a meaningful look. "Mel started it."

Carrie shrugged. "Actually, her mom kind of started it. See, I was just looking for an excuse to avoid hanging out with her, so I told everyone that I had to do math homework. Then Mrs. Eng was like, 'Oh—Mel's a math genius. She'll help you.'"

"And?" Sky prodded. She leaned forward, twirling her hair around her fingers.

"And . . . she came up to my room and made a point of calling me an idiot, like, a million times," Carrie lied. She smirked halfheartedly. "Of course, she's failing geography."

"She is?" Alex asked. "Now there's something I didn't know. I thought all The Amys were total brainiacs."

Carrie lowered her eyes, staring at the worn knees of her black corduroys. "Not all of them," she said quietly.

Alex shook her head. "So did she help you?"

"Are you kidding? I wouldn't let Mel Eng be my math tutor," she lied. "I'd rather fail eighth grade and be a social outcast."

"What other dirt did you find out?" Sky blurted impatiently.

Carrie paused. "Dirt?"

"Yeah. The dirt on Mel. You must know some more juicy gossip about her, right?" Sky cocked her eyebrow. "Or at least something good about Amy Anderson or Aimee Stewart?"

"Oh . . ." Carrie looked at her lap again.

Yesterday, she wouldn't have hesitated to make up something about Mel on the spot.

But now . . . now she couldn't. The only juicy gossip was that she and Mel Eng got along. Of course, that would qualify as "dirt" as far as her friends were concerned. That was the worst secret of all.

"Well?" Sky asked.

Carrie shook her head. "There's really nothing," she breathed.

"Mel wouldn't tell you anything, anyway," Alex said. "Why would she? You guys hate each other."

Carrie winced. She suddenly wished she were far away from this boat. It was crazy. These were her friends. But Alex's words made her very, very uncomfortable. She'd never felt more confused in her life.

She had thought that if she could just hang out with Alex and Sky and Jordan and Sam, everything would be fine. Life would be back to normal.

But life was *not* back to normal—not by a long shot.

Ten

Mel couldn't concentrate. It was a little scary. She never lost her focus when it came to planning the layout and story ideas for the *Robert Lowell Observer*. In three whole years of staying after school every other Tuesday to work on the newspaper with Amy and Aimee, she had always been razor sharp. They all had. That was why Principal Cashen had named the three of them joint editors-in-chief at the beginning of the semester.

It was a perfect situation: The most popular girls in school now controlled the *Robert Lowell Observer* from start to finish. Mel knew she couldn't have dreamed of anything better. She had the freedom to print pretty much whatever she wanted. So why couldn't she just shove her stupid personal problems aside and *enjoy* it?

". . . Hello . . . uh, Mel? Are you with us, Mel?"

Mel blinked and shook her head.

"Sorry," she murmured. "What was that?"

Amy and Aimee exchanged an annoyed glance. The three of them had been sitting cross-legged on the gray tile floor of the art studio for the past forty-five minutes, putting different sections of the paper together under the pale glow of fluorescent lights. But Mel hadn't been much help. She'd spent most of the time staring out the windows at the rain, trying to figure out how she would avoid going to the Mersels' house the next afternoon.

"Where do you think the sports page should go?" Aimee asked.

Mel shrugged. "I'm sorry. I . . . uh, guess I wasn't really listening."

"No duh." Aimee sat up straight and peered at Mel closely. "Are you all right?"

Mel lowered her eyes. "I'm just a little out of it," she mumbled.

"She's got PCSD," Amy announced.

"I've got *what?*" Mel asked, frowning.

"Post-Carrie Stress Disorder," Amy explained casually. A thin smile appeared on her lips. "It comes from spending too much time with a certain . . . shall we say, *garden*-variety loser. Symptoms include depression, a tendency to wig out for no apparent reason, becoming a space cadet—"

"All right, all right," Mel grumbled. "Very funny. Joke's over now."

Amy raised her eyebrows, glancing at Aimee. "Touchy, aren't we?"

"Well, excuse me," Mel said. Her tone was flat. "I thought we had better things to do than talk about Carrie Mersel."

Amy's steely blue eyes met hers. She blinked a few times. "We do," she said calmly. "We aren't the ones who are spacing out."

"I'm *sorry*, all right?" Mel growled. "Jeez . . . how many times do I have to say it?" She forced herself to look at the big blank sheets of newsprint spread out in front of them.

"You know, I noticed something," Amy said in a toneless voice. "You haven't said one word all day about yesterday's date with the Mersels. Don't you have anything to tell us?"

Mel didn't look up. Great. She knew this was going to happen sooner or later. She'd avoided it at lunch, because Amy had spent the whole time babbling about some cute guy she'd seen in a movie the afternoon before. But now . . .

"Carrie?" Amy prodded.

"There's nothing to tell, really," Mel mumbled. "I went to Carrie's house—and it was even more lame the second time around. End of story."

"Come on, Mel," Aimee whined. "Something must have happened."

Mel squeezed her eyes shut, then let out a deep breath. "I'm telling you, *nothing* happened. Carrie had to study for some math quiz. My mom—"

"Math quiz?" Amy interrupted. "But that's impossible. Carrie and I both have Mr. Engel. We didn't have any quiz in my class."

Mel opened her eyes. She couldn't believe this.

They actually thought she was lying. Now, of all times, when she was telling the truth.

"She was making it up," Mel explained slowly. "You know—to avoid hanging out with me. So my mom was like, 'Mel's a math whiz! She'll help you study.' Then Carrie had to admit she was lying, and we got into a fight, and I went home. My mom is making me go back there tomorrow. Satisfied?"

Neither of them said anything.

Mel breathed a secret sigh of relief. Finally.

"So," she went on after a minute. "We were talking about the sports page. . . ."

"Right," Amy replied in a very businesslike manner. "The sports page." She tossed her head back and yanked a fuzzy hairband out of her jeans pocket—then, in one single and amazingly graceful maneuver, she pulled her long blonde locks into a perfect ponytail. "I think we should scrap it altogether."

Mel's eyes narrowed. That made no sense.

"Uh . . . scrap it?" Aimee asked.

Amy leaned over the paper again. "That's right. I want to run a full-page ad instead."

"A full-page ad," Mel repeated blankly. She turned to Aimee, hoping for an explanation. But Aimee looked just as baffled as she did.

Amy glanced up and flashed them both a wicked grin. "I've got a plan."

Uh-oh. Mel knew that look on Amy's face all too

80

well. It usually came right before she suggested something totally outrageous.

"What is it?" Aimee whispered.

Amy took a deep breath. Mel couldn't remember the last time her friend had looked so pleased with herself. In spite of her foul mood, Mel actually found herself smiling, too. A full-page ad? This was going to be crazy. Mel was dying to know who the latest victim was.

"Well, I was thinking," Amy began slowly. "We never run any personals. You know: 'Eighth-grade geek seeks beautiful sixth-grade girl to share a lifetime of crossword puzzles, zit medicine, and polyester Hawaiian shirts.'"

Aimee's brow became slightly furrowed. "You want to run personals for losers?"

"Aimee, please," Amy scolded jokingly. "I think it's about time we reached out to Robert Lowell's romantically challenged students, don't you?" Her voice grew serious. "As editors-in-chief, we have a duty to serve the school community. That includes losers, doesn't it? We can't be prejudiced."

Mel smirked. "Right," she said. "And you really expect people to run personal ads? Do you know how embarrassing that would be?"

"You're absolutely right, Mel," Amy stated. "That's why we need to do it for them."

Mel stared at her. She started laughing. "Are you saying . . . ?"

"I'm saying that in the next issue of the *Robert Lowell Observer,* we're going to run a full-page personal ad that will feature a very special person making a very special request for love."

Aimee was giggling now, too. "Who?"

"Who do you think?" Amy raised her hands and looked Mel directly in the eye. "Mel's brand-new best friend. Carrie Mersel."

Eleven

Mel stopped laughing. "Carrie Mersel?" she repeated.

Amy didn't even blink. "Of course," she said simply. "Who else?"

Mel's stomach twisted queasily. She should have known. Whenever Amy had something up her sleeve these days, it was always directed at Carrie. After all, Carrie was Amy's biggest enemy. Mel had said those exact words to herself only yesterday. And she had sworn to herself that Carrie was her enemy, too. But pulling this kind of prank wouldn't do any good. Pranks like this only accomplished one thing in the long run: a full-fledged war. Amy and Carrie were almost at that stage already.

"Is there a problem?" Amy asked as innocently and politely as ever.

Mel hesitated. "Well, what are you planning to say in the ad, exactly?" she asked.

Amy chuckled. "I have it all figured out." She pointed to one of the big blank sheets of newsprint on the floor. "There's gonna be a huge photo of Carrie that takes up the entire page. Then there's gonna be a caption that says, 'Hi! I'm Carrie Mersel, and I'm really, really desperate for a man. This is no joke. So if you are male, under the age of seventy, and have an IQ of more than ten, I'll take you. As you can tell from the picture, weight is not an issue.'"

Mel's mouth fell open. She was too horrified to respond. That was sick.

Aimee clapped her hands delightedly. "That's awesome! Do you have a picture?"

"Not yet," she replied. She raised her eyes to Mel. "That's where you come in."

Mel was already shaking her head.

"Don't look so freaked, Mel," Amy teased. "It'll be easy. You just have to do one simple thing. Do the Mersels have any photographs of Carrie on their walls or in frames or anything?"

"How should I know?" she muttered dismally. "I never bothered to look."

Amy sighed. "Well, when you go over there tomorrow, *look*, all right? Because you're gonna have to grab a picture of her and sneak it out of her house. And try to look for a black-and-white one that was taken in the past few months if you—"

"No," Mel interrupted, glowering. "I am not going to steal something from the Mersels. Do you have any idea how much trouble I'd get into if I got caught?"

"You're *not* going to get caught," Amy mumbled irritably. "You're too smart to get caught."

"Amy, that—that's not even the point," Mel stammered. "Stealing is wrong, all right? I've never stolen anything before in my whole life."

But Amy just laughed. "You're not going to be stealing, Mel." She sounded as if she were talking to somebody incredibly stupid—like Jordan Sullivan or something. "You're gonna be borrowing. Just bring the photo in here so I can make a copy of it and blow it up for the paper. As soon as I'm done, you can take it back."

Mel didn't even answer. She was no longer nervous—she was angry. Did Amy really think she would "borrow" a picture of Carrie from the Mersels just so Amy could pull off the cruelest, most . . . low prank Mel had ever heard of? Well, she wasn't going to have any part in it. She didn't care what Amy thought.

"See, I knew these little get-togethers would come in handy," Amy continued. She had a smug and self-satisfied smile, as if nothing was wrong at all. "I actually got the idea yesterday at lunch, when you started telling me about what happened at that first visit. I mean, knowing that you were actually in Carrie's house, well, the possibilities—"

"Don't you think we're gonna get in trouble for putting a fake personal ad in the school paper?" Mel snapped.

Amy made a face. "Excuse me?"

"You heard me," Mel said. Her voice was quavering slightly.

"We're the editors-in-chief, Mel," Amy replied.

Her voice was cold. "We can do whatever we want."

"Yeah, Mel—what's your problem?" Aimee demanded. "Why are you wigging out?"

"Wigging *out?*" Mel cried. "You're the ones who are wigging out. A prank is one thing, but this is too much. Pranks are supposed to be funny. This isn't funny at all. It's just plain mean."

Amy's lips twitched. Her blue eyes were blazing. "You've got some nerve," she hissed.

Mel swallowed. "What? I'm telling you—"

"What about what Carrie did?" Amy spat. "She pasted that horrible picture of me up on my locker for the whole world to see the first week of school. Do you even have the slightest idea how embarrassing that was? What's the difference between what Carrie did to me and what we're going to do to her?"

Mel didn't answer. She knew that when Amy thought she was right, there was no point in arguing. But she was starting to get a little nervous. Amy was mad—probably more mad than Mel had ever seen her. Aimee was shaking her head in disappointment.

"What's wrong with you, Mel?" Amy's voice rose to a shout. "If you had any kind of backbone at all, you would—"

"It has nothing to do with backbone!" Mel yelled back.

Amy blinked once. Then she pushed herself to her feet. She jerked a finger toward the door. "I want you to leave," she stated quietly.

Mel just sat there and gaped up at her.

"I'm serious."

Mel shook her head. How did this happen? Why were they fighting—over this? "Amy . . ."

"You know, I guess your mom's little scheme worked," Amy said with a cruel smile. "You *are* friends with Carrie Mersel."

The color drained from Mel's face. *No . . .*

She felt sick. She couldn't believe it. Her worst nightmare was coming true—right here, right before her eyes. Amy did think Carrie had rubbed off on her.

"That's what happened, isn't it?" Amy whispered.

"No," Mel said in a hollow voice. Her throat was dry. "That's not what—"

"Don't even try it, Mel," Amy said dismissively. "You've always been a total softy. But the fact that you became friends with Carrie isn't even the point. The point is, we're going to pull a prank on her—whether you like it or not." She shrugged. "And we can't exactly discuss it if one of her friends is around, can we?"

Mel shook her head again, desperately. "I'm not her friend," she insisted.

"Whatever, Mel," Amy said in a dull voice. She waved her hand at the door again. "But you still gotta beat it."

Mel gave Aimee one last despairing look. But she knew it was hopeless. Aimee wouldn't even return her gaze. Besides, Aimee would never side with Mel over Amy—not in a million years. Aimee wouldn't side with herself over Amy. She lived for Amy Anderson, plain and simple.

"We're waiting," Amy said.

"What about the newspaper?" Mel croaked. Her eyes were starting to moisten.

"We'll finish it," Amy stated tonelessly. "Don't worry about that. You weren't much help to us today, anyway."

Mel opened her mouth one last time, but no words would come.

What could she say? She stumbled to her feet, sniffing. *Why are you doing this to me?* she wondered. *Why . . .*

"Oh yeah—Mel?" Amy said.

Mel hesitated. There was silence. Rain pounded incessantly against the windows. Still, one last tiny flame of hope flickered inside her.

"Be sure to shut the door on your way out."

Mel

Dear Diary,

So it's pouring rain right now, and I'm sitting here at my desk, and I think I might start crying.

But you want to know the crazy thing? I can't stop thinking about this cheesy eighties movie I once saw. I can't even remember the name of it. All I remember is that I was flipping through the channels on a rainy afternoon just like this one, and I ended up watching this really bad movie.

One scene keeps flashing through my mind. A really beautiful girl is having a fight with a really good-looking guy. I think they were fighting about money. It must have been about money, because they were both throwing a lot of expensive china at each other.

Anyway, the scene ends with the girl saying: "When you've

had money and lost it, it's a whole lot worse than not having had it at all."

That's _exactly_ the way I feel about popularity.

Just substitute the word ~~popularity~~ for ~~money~~, and I could have ~~been~~ the girl in that scene. The point is that in one incredibly stupid move, I lost my two best friends. I had it all — and now it's gone. Even the biggest losers at Robert Lowell are better off than I am. Everybody has _someone_. Everybody has at least one other person to talk to. But not me. I have nobody.

Okay, I still have Mr. Bubbles. But how pathetic is _that?_

I feel as though I should be angry at someone. I guess I _am_ angry at my mom. If my mom hadn't met Mrs. Mersel, none of this would have happened. But the truth is that I'm too depressed to be angry. Besides, if there's one thing I've learned, it's that you can't say "what if." Those two words never get you anywhere.

So now I have a decision to make.

Either I beg Amy to forgive me and go along with her prank, or I tell Carrie.

Neither of those choices is very appealing.

The thing I want most is to be friends with Amy again, obviously. And it's not even like the idea of a prank on Carrie bothers me all that much. I don't have any loyalty to Carrie.

No, it's the prank itself. I don't think it's fair. Having your picture in the school newspaper with the words "I desperately need a man" is <u>much</u> more embarrassing than anything that has happened to Amy — no matter what she says. It's the kind of thing that can really hurt someone. And I don't want to do that. Not to Carrie, not to anyone.

But one thing I do know is that I am _not_ going to give up my friendship with Amy. My friendship with Amy is the most important thing in the world.

So what am I going to do? How did I even get into this mess?

It doesn't matter. What matters is that Amy and I become friends again. And you know what? I'm pretty much prepared to do anything. That scares me.

It scares me because if things get worse, I might start thinking that Amy's prank _isn't_ so bad.

Wednesday:

Decisions, Decisions . . .

8:27 A.M. Mel boards the bus. Aimee boards a few seconds later—but sits in Amy's seat, without a glance in Mel's direction.

8:31 A.M. Amy boards the bus and sits next to Aimee. She ignores Mel, too. For the first time ever, Mel is alone on Bus #4.

8:32 A.M. Carrie boards the bus, casts a sidelong glance at Mel, and hurries to the backseat.

8:35 A.M. Sky boards the bus, stares confusedly at Mel for several seconds, then hurries to the backseat.

8:36 A.M. Sky wants to know why Mel isn't sitting with Aimee. She pesters Carrie about it until they get to school.

8:45 A.M. Aimee informs Amy that she brought a Polaroid camera to school today to take a certain girl's picture for a certain personal ad. Amy is extremely pleased.

10:15 A.M. Mel leaves a note in Amy's locker:

I'm so sorry about what happened yesterday. I acted like a jerk. I want to talk to you and

straighten this out before I
really wig out.

Mel

10:55 A.M. Amy finds Mel's note and stuffs it in her pocket.

11:03 A.M. Carrie listens in horror as Mr. Engel announces a "comprehensive" geometry exam for the following Friday.

11:41 A.M. Amy bumps into Aimee in the hall and shows her Mel's note. The two of them shake their heads. Doesn't Mel understand? She already has wigged out.

12:31 P.M. Sky wants to know if she can come over to Carrie's this afternoon and watch MTV. The cast members of *Friends* are going to be guest veejays. Carrie glumly informs her that she'll have to watch somewhere else. Carrie has plans—with the Engs.

12:32 P.M. Mel sits with Amy and Aimee. Neither of them says a word to her.

12:43 P.M. Carrie hangs her head in misery as Sky makes plans with Alex, Jordan, and Sam to watch MTV at Alex's house. Once again, she'll be missing out.

12:50 P.M. Amy and Aimee finish their lunches and leave the table without saying good-bye to Mel.

12:54 P.M. Sky instructs Carrie to use her visit with Mel to find out what's going on with The Amys. Carrie is briefly tempted to throw her applesauce in Sky's face.

94

1:35 P.M. Amy listens in horror as Mr. Engel announces a "comprehensive" geometry exam for the following Friday.

2:32 P.M. Mel goes to the girls' bathroom and flips a coin. Heads, she'll tell Carrie; tails, she'll go along with the prank. After five heads and five tails, she gives up.

3:14 P.M. Aimee wants to take Carrie's picture as soon as Carrie leaves the school building, but Amy can hardly think about the prank. She's way too freaked about the geometry exam.

3:15 P.M. Aimee snaps a bunch of photos anyway, just as Carrie dashes down the front steps to Bus #4.

Twelve

"This is so totally weird," Sky kept whispering as the bus rattled up Pike's Way. Her gaze was locked on Mel, as if she were a moth and the back of Mel's head were a giant hundred-watt lightbulb. "Mel is sitting by herself again. I can't get over it—"

"Will you give it a rest already?" Carrie moaned. "What's the big deal?"

Sky looked at her. Her eyes widened.

Carrie glanced around the backseat. Alex was looking at her, too. So were Sam and Jordan. Everyone was staring at her as if she were a lunatic. Great. Not only was she spending less and less time with her friends, but they all thought she was losing her mind.

"Sorry," she muttered. She managed a tired grin. "Look—maybe she's just embarrassed because she stained her shirt at lunch or something."

Jordan smiled. "Mel Eng's a slob?"

Carrie rolled her eyes.

"Listen, I'm sorry to keep harping on this Mel thing, Carrie," Sky said, leaning back into the seat. Her eyes wandered up the aisle again. "But I'm totally fascinated by it. You have to admit, this is epic in the history of Robert Lowell. The Amys have never, ever turned on each other. *Ever.*"

For a moment, Carrie was half tempted to say: *So?* But the truth was that she couldn't stop thinking about the "Mel thing," either. She just didn't want to admit why—to herself or to anyone else.

Part of it was guilt, of course. She was positive that the other Amys were dissing Mel because she was hanging out with Carrie. Amy probably thought that Mel's soul had been polluted from spending too much time with somebody who didn't have a J. Crew catalog. And even though Carrie knew she shouldn't have given a sack of horse poop about what The Amys thought, she didn't want to be responsible for ruining somebody's social life, either.

But the other reason—the scarier reason—was that she could see herself in Mel's position. She could see herself being shut out. What if Alex, Sky, Jordan, and Sam started to get suspicious of her? What if they thought that her personality was changing because she was hanging out with Mel so much? Would they still want to cram into the backseat with her every morning and afternoon? Maybe they wouldn't. Maybe she and Mel would wind up sitting together, staring out the window.

"You know, now that Mel's out of the picture, I think I'm gonna become one of The Amys," Jordan stated. "They could use a guy, and I think—"

Sky slapped him on the arm.

"Ow!" he yelped, laughing. "What? It makes perfect sense. I've got dirty blond hair and green eyes, just like Aimee Stewart. And I'm smooth-talking and slick, just like Amy—"

"You're just saying that because you have crushes on both of them," Sky interrupted with a smirk.

Jordan started shaking his head, but his face had turned slightly pink.

"Aha!" Sky teased. She nudged Carrie. "See! He's blushing. . . ."

Carrie tried to smile, but she couldn't. For some reason, she was beginning to feel empty again—the way she'd felt yesterday on Sky's boat. It didn't make any sense. She was here, with her friends. But she felt awkward, removed from the action. She almost felt as if she were watching a home movie of the four of them. Somehow, knowing she was about to miss out was just as bad as actually missing out.

"Enough with this crush stuff," Sam said in a deadpan voice from the other end of the seat. A few tufts of his spiky black hair poked out from behind Jordan. "I think I might puke. I don't want to imagine Jordan and Amy Anderson together. It's too gross. I mean, just picture what their kids would look like."

"Eww!" Sky whispered.

Alex laughed. "Yeah—they might look okay, but they'd be really horrible saxophone players who

98

spent all their time watching lame soap operas."

Jordan shook his head. "Man. You guys are so lost. If Amy Anderson and I had kids, they'd be the coolest kids on the block. They'd be sharply dressed, sharp-witted, amazing-looking basketball stars . . ." He stopped in midsentence.

A hush fell like a blanket over the backseat.

Carrie looked up. She hadn't even noticed—but the bus was already turning onto Whidbey Road.

Home at last, she thought grimly.

"See you guys later," she murmured. She slung her backpack over her shoulder and began the long march up the aisle.

"Bye, Carrie," they called in unison.

Carrie shook her head. Even that was depressing. Her friends sounded like four parts of the same being—not four separate people. She kept hoping she wouldn't have to say anything to Mel. But she needn't have worried. Mel leaped up and bolted out before Carrie was even halfway to the door.

"Have fun!" Aimee said brightly as Carrie walked past her.

Carrie paused on the stairs, turned, and flashed her a wide smile. "Drop dead!" she cried, mimicking Aimee's voice.

"Hey," Brick protested. "That's not . . ."

But Carrie hurried up the driveway before Brick could finish. Mel wouldn't even look at her as the two of them made their way to the front door. Of

99

course, Carrie wasn't surprised that Mel wasn't too happy. She didn't have any friends anymore.

Carrie was not going to let that happen to her though. Today she was going to do something so awful, so ill-mannered, so offensive that Mel and Mrs. Eng would never want to set foot in this house again.

She wasn't sure yet what it would be—but she'd think of something. She didn't have a choice.

Thirteen

"Hi, you two!" Mrs. Mersel sang out from the kitchen. She strode into the front hall. "So what do you think . . . ?"

Carrie's jaw dropped. She didn't know whether to laugh or to call the nearest mental institution. For a second, she even forgot about Mel. Her mom was wearing a pair of faded jeans, an old sweatshirt, and some ridiculous shiny rubber boots. Her long blonde hair was actually pulled back into a ponytail. Carrie wouldn't have believed this was her mother if she hadn't been standing in her own home.

"So?" Mrs. Mersel prodded hopefully. "Do I look like a real gardener? Give me your honest opinion now, Carrie."

"I'm . . . uh, speechless," Carrie muttered. She shot a quick glance at Mel. But Mel didn't seem to care. Then again, Mel had no idea that Elizabeth Mersel hadn't worn anything but the latest businesswear since the late seventies.

"I'll take that as a yes," Carrie's mom said with a satisfied smile.

"Hi, girls," Mrs. Eng called from the living room.

Carrie wrenched her eyes away from her mother. Mel's mom looked bizarre, too. What was going on here? Mrs. Eng was wearing a grubby pair of sweatpants and a flannel shirt—and the same type of shiny and totally absurd rubber boots that Carrie's mom was wearing.

At least now Mel was shocked—or amused, anyway.

"Um, are you gardening in our backyard or something?" Carrie asked as Mrs. Eng joined them in the hall.

"As a matter of fact, we're on our way out the door," Mrs. Mersel said. She grabbed her purse off the glass end table in the front hall and slung it over her shoulder. "There's a—"

"Wait a minute," Carrie interrupted, totally bewildered. "You're leaving?"

"Yes, dear," her mom said matter-of-factly. "Today we're learning how to plant herbs. And we really must get going. We're due at Celia Tucker's house in Tacoma in less than an hour."

"But—but I thought the garden club met on Thursdays," Carrie stammered. This was insane. They couldn't leave. How was Carrie supposed to offend Mrs. Eng and her own mom if they weren't even here?

Mrs. Mersel shrugged. "There's a chance it might rain tomorrow, so we all decided to have our lesson a day early—"

"You're going all the way to Tacoma?" Mel cried, finally opening her mouth for the first time. "What are *we* supposed to do for the whole afternoon?"

"Calm down, Melissa," her mom said firmly. "You two will be just fine."

"Don't you see? This is the best possible situation for all of us." Mrs. Mersel flashed both Carrie and Mel a brief smile. "You two can make a fresh start. You'll have the house to yourselves for the next few hours. Why don't you watch a video? Or you can surf the Net or . . ."

Carrie couldn't listen. One thought kept running through her mind: Her plan was ruined, and this nightmare would never end.

". . . And there's plenty of food in the fridge," Mrs. Mersel concluded. She pushed the door open, letting Mrs. Eng out first. "So have fun!"

"Fun?" Carrie croaked. Her mom sounded exactly like Aimee Stewart.

"I'll be back by eight o'clock, Melissa," Mrs. Eng said with a backward wave over her shoulder.

Mel shook her head. "But—"

The door swung shut.

Carrie took a deep breath. It had all happened so fast—too fast to fully grasp the reality of the situation.

She turned to Mel, gazing at her hideous beige turtleneck sweater and matching beige pants. She couldn't be standing here by herself with Mel Eng. It was too crazy.

This has to be some terrible cosmic joke. . . .
But it wasn't.

Carrie was stuck with Mel for the rest of the afternoon and evening . . . and probably the rest of her life, too.

Fourteen

For a few long moments, the two of them stood in the silent peach-and-white-checkered hall and stared at each other.

Finally Carrie shook her head. "How could they leave us here like this?" she breathed.

Mel looked at the floor. "Well, there's nothing we can do about it now," she said quietly.

"I guess you have a point," Carrie replied in a strained voice. She slipped off her backpack, then tossed it onto the stairs and forced herself to walk toward the kitchen. *You are not going to freak out*, she commanded herself. *You are just going to pretend like nothing is wrong.*

"Are you hungry at all?" she asked as politely as she could. "I think we have—"

"Carrie, wait."

She froze in her tracks. There was a harsh edge in Mel's voice. What was her problem? Provoking each other wouldn't do either of them any good. It was tense enough in here already. Besides, nobody would be around to witness a fight.

"What?" Carrie asked flatly.

"I . . . uh, I wanted to give you back *The Shining*," Mel said. She didn't sound mad, but she didn't sound overly friendly, either. "I think . . . you should have it back."

Carrie glanced over her shoulder. Mel was crouched down on the floor, rifling through her backpack. After a few seconds, she pulled out the worn paperback and held it up in front of her as if it were poison.

"Here," she said.

Carrie didn't move at first. Why was Mel giving her back the book now? It didn't make much sense—considering the circumstances. If anything, Mel should have held on to it so she'd have something to do for the next few hours.

"Are you done with it?" Carrie asked.

Mel shook her head. "No."

Carrie frowned. "So why—"

"I just want you to *have* it, all right?" Mel stood up and shoved the book into Carrie's hands. "Do I have to explain every little thing I do to you?"

Mel's face was now less than a foot from Carrie's. And Carrie could tell right then that something serious was bothering her—something way more important than the book . . . and maybe even something worse than being stuck in this house with Carrie. Mel's lips were twitching as if she was trying to stop herself from crying. Her forehead was creased. . . .

The Amys.

Of course. Carrie had been so rattled by her mom that she'd forgotten the obvious. Mel blamed her for all her problems. Mel blamed her for getting dumped by Amy and Aimee.

"Look, Mel," Carrie said carefully, taking the book. "I'm sorry if, you know . . . if this whole thing with our mothers has caused any problems between you and your friends." She lowered her eyes. "But you shouldn't blame me—"

Mel suddenly laughed.

Carrie made a face. "What?"

Mel didn't answer right away. She just sighed hopelessly, then marched into the living room. "Forget it. You have no idea what you're even talking about," she muttered.

"What is *that* supposed to mean?" Carrie demanded.

Mel plopped herself down onto the peach couch and stared morosely at the carpet. "It's just that 'this whole thing'—as you call it—is much more complicated than you realize."

"Complicated?" Carrie stood in the hall, glaring at her. Mel wasn't making any sense at all.

"Anyway," Mel said quietly, "it doesn't even matter anymore."

"*What* doesn't matter?" Carrie cried. "Will you stop acting like a jerk and tell me?"

Mel glanced up at her and opened her mouth, then

quickly closed it. She chewed her lip. Then she took a deep breath and said, "Let me ask you something, Carrie. What's the worst thing you would do to get back at somebody for something bad they did to you?"

Carrie took a step back. Whoa. Where had that come from? The worst thing Carrie would do . . . What kind of a question was that? It sounded like the kind of thing a demented killer would say in a made-for-TV movie. This conversation was actually starting to give her the creeps.

"Well?" Mel asked.

"I didn't know we were playing 'Truth or Dare,'" Carrie mumbled.

Mel shook her head. She fidgeted restlessly on the couch—fiddling one moment with the hem of her turtleneck, the next with the crease in her pants—never keeping still for more than an instant. "Believe me, it's not a game. Just answer the question," she insisted.

"I . . . I don't know," Carrie stammered clumsily. "It's not like I have a ready-made answer or anything. Why do you want to know?"

"Because it's important," Mel stated.

"Well, it's important to me to know why you're asking such a weird question," Carrie replied hotly. She tossed *The Shining* onto the long glass table in the hall—mostly to avoid looking Mel in the eye. "You're making me nervous."

Mel walked back into the hall and stood behind Carrie. "You should be nervous."

Carrie whirled to face her. "Why?" she cried.

"Because Amy and Aimee are pulling a prank on you in the next couple of days. And it's gonna be bad."

Fifteen

Carrie gasped. So that's what this was all about.

"Wait, hold on," she said, raising her hands. A sickening feeling gripped her insides. She needed a second to think. "How do you . . ." Her voice trailed off. "Are you sure?"

Mel's gaze fell to the floor again. "Of course I'm sure." She shook her head. "But I didn't even know until right this second if I was going to tell you or not."

Carrie drew in her breath. She did have a reason to be nervous. She chewed on a black-painted fingernail. "Is that why you asked me what *I* would do to get back at somebody?"

Mel nodded. "See—listen, you have to understand . . . it's got nothing to do with you."

"It doesn't?" Carrie asked, wrinkling her brow. "Then who does it have to do with?"

"No, no, I didn't mean it like that." She frowned. "It's just . . . they're planning on putting a picture of you in the school paper. They're gonna make it like a personal ad. There's gonna be a caption that says something like: 'I'm Carrie Mersel, and I'm ugly, and

I'm totally desperate, and I'll take any man, no matter how gross. Please call.' And they're definitely gonna do it, too. Nobody can stop them."

Carrie swallowed.

"It's true," Mel said.

Oh, jeez. This was bad, all right. If what Mel was saying was true, Carrie would never be able to set foot in Robert Lowell again without being the laughingstock of the entire school. Nope, she'd have to get radical plastic surgery and go into hiding.

"Why are you even telling me?" she asked. "I mean, if there's nothing I can do . . ."

"Because I think it's mean," Mel said simply. "That's what I meant when I said it has nothing to do with you. To be honest, I don't care what happens to you. I just don't think something like this should happen to anyone—no matter how much of a loser she is."

Carrie pursed her lips. Well, well, well. That was a really beautiful thing to say. "Thanks a lot," she murmured.

"You *should* thank me." Mel began pacing agitatedly from the hall to the living room and back. "Look, Carrie. The truth is that if they'd come up with something else, I would have gone along with it, all right? You deserve a good prank."

Carrie laughed dryly. In a weird way, she couldn't exactly blame Mel for saying that. She could almost see Mel's point of view. After all, there was no denying that Carrie had pulled more than a few stunts on Mel and her best friends. Good ones, too.

Mel paused in midstep. "What's so funny?" she demanded.

"Nothing," Carrie mumbled.

"Well, I'm really, really glad you think this is so amusing," Mel said sarcastically. "Thanks to you, I may have lost my best friends."

Carrie snorted. "That's not my fault. *I* didn't force you to do anything. You could have gone along with them. It was your choice."

Mel gaped at her. She blinked a few times very rapidly, then turned away. "Don't you understand?" she whispered.

Understand what? Carrie thought. *That you take pity on "losers"?* She didn't even bother to answer. But Mel was trembling now, standing with her back to Carrie and her arms wrapped tightly around her sides. She sniffed once loudly.

Oh, brother.

As angry and fed up as Carrie was, she didn't want to make Mel cry. She supposed she should have been thankful for the fact that Mel hadn't gone along with the prank. But why? The Amys were still going to get her. And Mel hadn't acted out of any loyalty or goodwill. No, Mel had made her position on their relationship perfectly clear when she said: "I don't care what happens to you."

So much for the fledgling friendship. At this point, Carrie couldn't believe she had even considered the possibility that she could get along with Mel Eng.

"I gotta get out of here," Mel whispered. She started rubbing her eyes. "I can't be stuck here until eight o'clock."

"Well, why don't you just go to Amy's house?" Carrie said. "She only lives like two blocks away. Seriously. Just go there, and when your mom comes back, I'll tell her that we got in a fight and you went to hang out with your real friends."

Mel turned around. "Are you nuts?"

"What?" Carrie shrugged. At first, she was only semijoking, but the more she thought about it, the more she realized that it really wasn't such a bad idea. She didn't want Mel to hang around any more than Mel did. "If you've got problems with Amy, now's a perfect time to patch things up. I won't stand in your way."

Mel sniffed again. "What about the prank?"

"What about it? If you can talk your friends out of it, great. If not, I'll deal with it," Carrie said. "I'm sure I'll think of something."

"I don't want to tell them I told you," Mel said quietly.

Carrie snickered. "Fine. You think I want to tell my friends about this conversation? Or any conversation we've had?" She shook her head. "This works both ways, Mel. I want our lives to go back to normal. I feel the same way you do. I wish this had never happened. So you can walk out the door, and we can just forget about all the visits and the phone call—"

"And how I borrowed *The Shining*," Mel interrupted.

Carrie rolled her eyes. "Sure. Whatever. The point is that nothing we ever talked about has to leave this house. I don't want to lose my friends any more than you want to lose yours."

Mel nodded. "You're right." She marched determinedly into the hall and gathered up her backpack. "I don't want to lose my friends." She paused. "Just tell my mom . . ."

"I'll take care of it," Carrie mumbled. "Don't worry."

Mel put her hand on the doorknob. For the briefest instant, their eyes locked. But this time there was no smile between them. Mel opened the door.

"Bye, Carrie," she said.

"Bye, Mel."

The next moment, she was gone—out of Carrie's house and, Carrie hoped, out of her life forever.

Sixteen

Mel stepped back and forth across the flat concrete stoop of Amy's huge white house for what must have been the hundredth time. She just hoped none of the neighbors were watching her. She must have looked like a major loony-toon. But she couldn't bring herself to even peek at the doorbell. What if she rang and Amy just slammed the door in her face? What if—

No. She was not going to say "what if."

Finally, she reached for the doorbell with a trembling finger—but at the last second, her hand fell back to her side. She could just go back to Carrie's place. . . .

What was she thinking? Of course she couldn't go crawling back there. She wouldn't be able to live with herself if she did. Besides, she knew she'd be saying "what if" for the rest of her life if she lost her nerve right now. She was here. She was going to face Amy.

Just get it over with! she commanded herself.

She lifted her finger again and jabbed the glowing orange button.

After a few seconds, Mel heard the muffled sound

of pattering footsteps somewhere inside the house.

"Who is it?" Amy called.

Mel opened her mouth. But her heart was suddenly pounding too hard for her to speak. She licked her dry lips and forced herself to take a deep breath. "Mel," she answered feebly.

The door flew open.

"Amy, I . . ."

Mel left the sentence hanging. She had been planning to apologize before she even set foot in the house. But she hadn't been expecting Amy to be so friendly. Amy was standing there, looking as happy as could be, with the afternoon sun glistening in her bright blue eyes and her lips curled in a big, toothy smile.

"Am I glad to see you!" Amy exclaimed.

Mel blinked. This had to be some kind of cruel joke. Amy had spent the entire day treating Mel like an annoying stain that needed to be wiped off the face of Robert Lowell Middle School. Now she was glad to see her? Amy hardly ever said anything that nice—even when she *wasn't* mad. Maybe she was just trying to lull Mel into thinking that everything was fine before she turned and walked away.

"Hello, Mel—are you there?" Amy teased. "Anybody home?"

Mel swallowed. "I don't understand," she breathed hoarsely.

Amy raised her eyebrows. "About what?"

"You wouldn't even talk to me today."

"Oh, *that*." Amy waved her hand dismissively. "Forget about it. You were right. The prank is too mean. Plus, we don't have a picture. We took these Polaroids of Carrie today when she was getting on the bus, and none of them came out."

Mel's eyes widened. Was that it? Amy had forgiven her and called off the prank—just like that? Was it really that simple? It couldn't be so easy. . . .

Amy squinted at her. "Are you all right?"

Mel nodded. A long trembling sigh escaped her lips. Then she started giggling.

"What's so funny?" Amy asked.

Mel shrugged. She knew she looked foolish—but she couldn't stop. She'd never felt more relieved in her entire life. But she should have known Amy would forgive her. That was the great thing about Amy. She was the most fickle person Mel knew—in good ways and bad. And that meant she could never stay mad at one person for very long, least of all one of her best friends.

"Well," Amy said, stepping aside, "as soon as you're done laughing, you can catch the last five minutes of *Days of Our Lives*. My mom taped it for us."

Mel shook her head, managing to get a grip on herself. "Thanks," she murmured. She followed Amy through the hall and up the stairs. Her knees were still a little wobbly. She just hoped she wouldn't do anything majorly stupid—like start crying or something.

But there was still something she had to tell Amy—just to put an end to this whole crazy incident once and for all. She paused outside the closed door of the TV room at the end of the hall. "Amy . . ."

"What?" Amy asked.

Mel bit her lip. "Look . . . just so you know, I'm not friends with Carrie, okay?"

Amy nodded. "I know you aren't," she said gently. "You're here, aren't you?" She pushed open the door.

Mel smiled. So that was that. Carrie Mersel was out of her life for good. *Now* she could relax. She followed Amy through the doorway.

Then she froze.

Aimee was here, too. She was sitting on the couch, staring at the jumbo television as the closing credits of *Days of Our Lives* rolled across the screen. For a moment, Mel felt another twitter of anxiety. Had Aimee also forgiven her? Probably—if Amy had. Still . . .

"Who rang the doorbell?" Aimee asked distractedly.

"See for yourself," Amy said.

Aimee glanced up. Her face twisted into a scowl. "What's she—"

"Aimee, we both agreed that the prank was too mean, *didn't* we?" Amy stated, cutting Aimee off in midsentence. "We both agreed that Mel was right."

Mel gulped. So Aimee hadn't forgiven her. No . . .

for once in Aimee's life, it looked as if she didn't agree with Amy at all.

"The prank's out of the question, anyway," Amy went on. "The pictures you took were way too lame."

Aimee's cheeks reddened.

"Weren't they?" Amy pressed.

Aimee looked at the floor, but she nodded grudgingly. "I guess you're right," she said after a moment.

"Show Mel," Amy instructed.

Aimee sighed, then reached into the back pocket of her jeans and pulled out a few crumpled Polaroids. She shoved them in Mel's direction. "They're really bad," she mumbled. "So you don't need to say anything."

Mel took the photos and began flipping through them. Aimee was right. They were really bad. All she could see was a bunch of blurry human-shaped smudges. These were supposed to be pictures of Carrie? She couldn't even tell if Carrie was in any of them.

"Aimee, I know this is totally rude, but I'm gonna have to ask you to leave," Amy suddenly announced.

"*What?*" Aimee cried.

Mel glanced up from the pictures. What was going on here?

Amy smiled apologetically. "It's just that you know I have this dumb geometry exam on Friday," she said. She picked up the remote control from the couch and flicked off the TV. "And I'm, like, completely wigging out about it. My mom will kill me if I mess up." Her eyes wandered over to Mel. "So it's really kind of lucky that Mel showed up."

Mel felt a smile spreading across her face. Of course.

That's why Amy was so glad to see her.

But what did it matter? If anything, it showed that nothing had changed. Amy needed help with math—just like she always did. And if a little geometry exam was enough to make Amy forget about their fight, then that was fine with Mel.

"You don't mind helping me a little, do you?" Amy asked innocently.

Mel shook her head. She handed the photos back to Aimee. "Not one bit. You can always count on me. Always."

Amy smiled—that sweet, embracing smile that drew people to her like a magnet. "I know I can," she said. "That's why you're the only Mel who could ever be an Amy."

Heather's mother burst into the room. Her eyes glowed with a fiery, demonic light. Her blood-red lips were curled in a fiendish smile.

"What do you want?" Heather asked in a trembling voice.

"There's somebody I want you to meet," her mother whispered. "She's right here."

Heather shook her head. "No . . ."

"Oh yes," her mother replied. She took a step closer to the foot of Heather's bed. Her purplish nails were outstretched. "You're eighteen now. It's time you met somebody your age who has already been initiated."

Heather desperately backed away, pushing herself against the satin sheets, trying to somehow escape her mother. But there was nowhere to go. She was trapped.

"What do you mean . . . initiated?" Heather gasped.

"She's one of us. A witch . . ."

Seventeen

"Hi, Mel! Hi, Carrie! We're home!"

Carrie looked up from her typewriter.

Uh-oh.

"Where are you?" Mrs. Mersel called.

"I . . . uh, I'll be right down," Carrie stuttered. She glanced at the clock. It was seven forty-five. Wow. *That's* why it was so dark. She hadn't even thought about the time. And she didn't know how she was going to explain why Mel wasn't here anymore.

"What have you two been doing this whole time?" Mrs. Eng asked as cheerfully as ever.

Carrie leaped out of her chair. "Uh . . . I gotta tell you . . ." She ran a hand through her hair. Tell her what? Two pairs of heavy footsteps were pounding up the stairs. *Think!* she ordered herself. But her brain was taking a snooze. All she could think about were those dumb shiny boots, getting closer and closer. . . .

"Melissa?" Mrs. Eng called.

There was a loud knock on the door.

"Carrie?" Mrs. Mersel asked.

Carrie hung her head. She'd have to make up something on the spot. "Come in," she mumbled.

The door creaked open, revealing the "gardeners."

"Carrie, what are you two doing in here?" her mother asked with a laugh. "I can't see three inches in front of my face." She snapped on the light.

Carrie squinted at the two of them. They were still dressed in the same silly outfits—only now they were filthy from head to toe. Carrie was actually a little annoyed. Her mom hated it when *she* tracked dirt around the house. She took a deep breath. "Mom, before you say anything, I just have to—"

"Melissa?" Mrs. Eng asked, stepping into Carrie's room. She peered around curiously, then looked at Carrie. "Where's Melissa?"

Carrie shrugged. A dozen possible answers flashed through her brain—but there was really only one she could give. "Uh . . . she's at Amy Anderson's house."

Mrs. Eng flinched. *"What?"*

"Amy Anderson's house?" Mrs. Mersel cried. "What on earth is she doing there?"

"How should I know?" Carrie muttered, unable to think of any reasonable excuse. "She just took off. . . ."

Mrs. Eng was staring at Carrie. Her bright black eyes were suddenly very cold. "I'm sorry, young lady," she snapped. "But Mel would not just take off. Why don't you tell us what really happened."

"What really happened?" Carrie's voice rose slightly. "I just told you." She was starting to get a little angry herself. Who did Mrs. Eng think she was? She had no right to accuse Carrie of lying. Of course,

Carrie was lying, but that wasn't the point. The point was that Mrs. Eng's precious daughter was just as much to blame as she was.

"Did you two get into another fight?" Mrs. Mersel asked. "What time did she leave?"

"What did you *do*, Carrie?" Mrs. Eng asked insistently.

Carrie's gaze shifted between the two of them. She felt as if she were being questioned by the police. It was ridiculous. They were treating Carrie like an archvillain, just because Mel had gone over to her friend's house. What was the big deal, anyway?

"Let me ask *you* something," she said. "Was this what you two had in mind when you wanted Mel and me to be friends?"

Mrs. Mersel threw her grimy hands in the air. "Of course not! What kind of a question—"

"Because you should have learned the very first time you put us together that this was not going to work out," Carrie interrupted. "We don't get along. We've never gotten along. And we sure aren't gonna start now, just to please you. That's why Mel left."

For the first time all day, Carrie felt satisfied. She'd told the truth. And it was probably the first entirely honest thing she'd said about Mel since the whole "friends" thing started.

Mrs. Mersel's hands fell to her sides. She shook her head with disgust. "I don't know what's gotten into you. . . ."

"You still haven't answered the question, Carrie," Mrs. Eng stated, folding her arms across her chest. "What did you *do?*"

"I didn't *do* anything!" Carrie yelled. "Mel said that she didn't want to be stuck here until eight o'clock. So I told her to go hang out at Amy's house. Amy is her friend. I'm not. If you don't believe me, ask her yourself."

"Carrie, please," Mrs. Mersel pleaded. Her face was flushed. "Where are your manners?"

Carrie laughed shortly. "*My* manners!" She thrust a finger at Mel's mom. "What about *hers?*"

Mrs. Mersel clasped her hands over her mouth. For a moment, Carrie thought she might keel over from shock. Well, this was a royal disaster. Then again, she'd succeeded at one thing. She'd definitely done a good job of offending them both. One look at Mrs. Eng's sour smile was proof of that. But that *was* her original plan, anyway, wasn't it?

"You've obviously got a lot of growing up to do, young lady," Mrs. Eng breathed.

"Maybe you're right," Carrie said. She sighed tiredly. "But in that case, why would you want me to hang out with Mel in the first place? I mean, she's obviously much more grown-up than I am, right?"

Mrs. Mersel whimpered. Her hands were now covering her entire face.

"I'm not going to stand here and argue with a thirteen-year-old girl," Mrs. Eng growled. She turned to face Carrie's mom. "I'm sorry this didn't work out,

Elizabeth. But I think it would be best if our daughters didn't spend any more time together."

"What do you think we've been trying to tell you for the past week? *Jeez!*" Carrie marched over to her bed and collapsed facedown on the mattress.

"I am so sorry," Mrs. Mersel murmured.

Carrie heard feet shuffling. There was some hushed conversation on the stairs—but Carrie couldn't catch any of it. Of course, she didn't really care what they were saying—as long as Mel never came back.

The front door slammed.

Finally.

Carrie rolled over on her back. Well, she'd gotten Mel Eng out of her life. Now she just needed to get her friends back in. Sighing, she reached for the phone on her night table and dialed Alex's number.

The line rang twice, then somebody picked up.

"Hello?" Alex answered.

"Hey. It's me."

"Hey, what's up?" Alex asked eagerly. "How'd it go today? Did you survive all right?"

Carrie smiled. For the first time all week, she felt as if she was right where she belonged. Life was back to normal. The Amys were probably planning on getting her with some terrible prank, as always. Her mom was majorly angry, as always. And most importantly, nothing stood in the way of her and her friends.

"Alex," Carrie said. "You'll never guess what happened. . . ."

Mel

Dear Diary,

What a day. Mom just finished grounding me for the next week. But honestly? I'm kind of relieved. I thought I was going to be grounded for a month. I don't think I'll ever forget the look on my mom's face when she pulled up in front of Amy's house tonight. She was one seriously unhappy woman.

But in a crazy way, I was happy she was mad. Because at long last, she gave up on trying to make me be friends with Carrie. I guess Carrie said a bunch of really rude things to her. Of course, Mom blamed _me_. It boggles the mind. She said _I_ must have given Carrie a reason for wigging out. Mom always finds a way to make _me_ responsible for things I can't control.

Oh, well. Who cares? I have my best friends again. I'm one of The Amys again. I rule Robert Lowell again. And I'm never going to have to say another word to Carrie Mersel for the rest of my life.

I do have to make a confession, though. I'm really glad that Amy didn't pull that prank on Carrie. I kind of hope she just forgets about Carrie. It's not that I _like_ Carrie. It's just that I don't want to be mean to her. I don't want to be mean to anybody.

Maybe if life were a whole lot different, Carrie and I would be friends. Maybe if there were no one else on the planet except the two of us and Stephen King, Carrie and I would get along great. But thinking about something dumb like that is just another way of saying "what if."

And you know what? I _hate_ saying "what if."